LAZARUS

Nancy Swing

PARK PLACE PUBLICATIONS
Pacific Grove, California

First trade paperback edition November 2018
Designed by Patricia Hamilton
Manufactured in the United States of America

Published by
Park Place Publications
Pacific Grove, California
www.parkplacepublications.com

ISBN: 978-1-943887-76-7
Printed in U.S.A.

⌒

Cover photo: Shutterstock —Doug McLean

For Zaccaria

Books By Nancy Swing

Malice on the Mekong 2016

The Lewiston, West Virginia Trilogy
Child's Play 2017
Lazarus 2018
The Silver Foxes, coming in 2019

Author's Foreword

We lived in an old stone farmhouse in Italy for fifteen years, ten of them with a wonderful German Shepherd named Zaccaria. He was a bit of a rescue dog, clearly been abused and way too hungry. The first time I set down his dish, he knocked me over in his rush to eat. But he was very, very smart, as all German Shepherds are, and it took him about three days to learn the food would always come and no one would ever hit him again. When he misbehaved, he got The Voice, and he truly knew what that meant, hanging his head and looking like he was totally ashamed. He came to love and trust us but never anyone else except our beloved Graziano, who worked with us on gardens and fences and olives and fruit trees twice a week. Inevitably, Zaccaria lived out his life and had to be put to sleep when old age took away any ability he had to live a normal life. Not long after, Graziano suffered an agonizing death from cancer. Within a few weeks, I had a terrifying nightmare, so real I woke up, heart beating so hard against my ribs I had trouble breathing. Husband Russell was overseas, and I was alone, unable to get back to sleep. I wrote down the notes that finally became *Lazarus*, an homage to Zack but also to Aika and Jada, the three Shepherds in my life.

* * * * * *

A note about dialect: It's always a challenge to depict a character who speaks in regional dialect. Some readers may be offended by what they perceive as a condescending stereotype, others turned off by the effort to understand what the character is saying. The received wisdom from the literary world is to give a taste of dialect, but not to spell every word as it would be pronounced. For example, many Americans now substitute "-in" for "-ing" in word endings. But the punctuation is distracting in print, so it's standard practice to write "amazing" instead of "amazin'" and have faith that the reader will know how the word would be pronounced. I've listened to trusted readers of my second draft and profited from their suggestions about how my main character would talk. But ultimately I had to take some tough decisions to give you the flavor of Jimmy Lee's speech. I hope you'll be able to read it with ease and not be offended by my attempt to reproduce a voice that is dear to me.

A note about the cover photo: I looked at scores of stock photos of cabins, but I couldn't find one that matched my vision of Miz Simmons' place. I was about to give up when this one appeared to convey the feeling of the story, if not the actual cabin. And somehow, that just seemed right.

ACKNOWLEDGMENTS

This book in particular required a lot of help in order to ensure that I got fundamental details right. Heartfelt thanks to:

- Three West Virginia guys who did their best to keep me honest about facts, current practices, dialect, guns and how a sixteen year-old boy might see his world: Bob Swiger, Rick Wilson and another who wishes to remain anonymous. Special thanks to Bob for long ago suggesting I bring Eden and Bethanne back into the ongoing story of the folks who live in Lewiston, WV.
- Karl Anderson, DVM and Lori Anderson, RVT for veterinary and physiology advice.
- Attorneys William E. Gagen on trial law and Theresa McGuire on estate law for their generous pro bono counsel.
- Bill Picket at Ace Hardware, who spent a lot of time educating me about chains.
- Joyce Krieg, author and editor extraordinaire, for kindly answering weird questions about punctuation in this era when almost anything goes.
- Nick McGinnis and Terry Piotrkowski, two of the most thoughtful and helpful readers any author could ask for.

As always, any errors or shortcomings in *Lazarus* are mine alone.

* * * * * *

None of my books could have been written without the support of Russell Sunshine, fellow author, exceptional critic and life partner. In the end, all these books are really for him.

1

I SMELLED THE SMOKE BEFORE I hardly got over the ridge, even though it was wintertime. The heater in Dad's old truck only worked on high, so I had the window open a crack, and that terrible smell come in to torment my nostrils. Not just wood in that fire, but electrical and plastic too, and something worse, like a barbecue out of control.

I gunned the motor as fast as I could go on that crooked mountain road. Been one of them early West Virginia snows, a couple sloppy inches on the ground, coating bushes and tree limbs. But thank the Lord, the roads was just wet, not slick.

The further I got down into the holler, the more I knew what I feared was right. Miz Simmons' cabin was on fire. That ancient place we spent all summer and fall fixing up so she could live there in peace. And now that peace was up in flames.

I hit the remote for her high metal gate and drove through so fast the tires fishtailed in the gravel. The smoke was strong, made my eyes water. But I could still see what I didn't wanna see. The whole place was ablaze, fire coming outta the front door and through the windows, even up the chimney.

I jumped outta the truck, praying to Jesus. "Lord, is Miz Simmons inside? Help me find the strength to save her. Help me, Lord, help me."

But deep down, I knew the time for praying was gone. I couldn't get nowhere near the doors, front or back. Even them thick old logs was on fire. Then the roof fell in, just like it was the first time I saw it all them months ago. But this was from fire, not neglect. Course that did it. If Miz Simmons was inside, she was with the Lord, and it was too late to save her.

Tears run down my cheeks, and not just 'cause of the smoke. Sobs thumped my chest, and I fell to my knees. "I'm not sure, Lord, but I think she's gone, a woman who took in the lost and give 'em a home. Receive her into your grace and shower her with love everlasting. Amen."

Then I pulled out my cell, dialed 9-1-1 and told 'em to send a firetruck and the police. Plus an ambulance to take away a body.

The men in our volunteer fire department always act like they really care. They got there quick and set to work. Some of 'em hooked up the hoses to get the fire out, and others grabbed tools to keep it from spreading through the woods and up the ridge. That early November snow was helping, everything wet and not so likely to take light, even from them fierce flames. Them men chopped and dug a clear space all round, ruining all we done to make that land fruitful. But what did it matter now Miz Simmons was gone?

Even Sheriff Price—and I didn't think much of him—seemed stunned by what he saw and ready to take up some kinda investigation. Course I knew what happened, but I wasn't gonna tell Jerry Price. I didn't trust him to do what was right. Just told him about smelling the smoke and finding the place on fire.

It took hours, and I tried to stay outta everybody's way. Needed to feel Eden's arms round me in the worst way, but that wasn't gonna happen for a long while. Finally, them hardworking men was able to get inside, and they found Miz Simmons' body on the bed. I backed off as far as I could go, cause I didn't wanna see that dreadful sight. I wanted to remember her alive, just like she was yesterday and all the days before. I didn't kneel down again, but I started praying that she didn't feel a thing. I wanted her to been knocked out by that medicine she took for her terrible headaches.

Finally, almost everybody was gone. Sheriff Price made me promise to come in and make an official statement, and I asked if I could go round behind them ruins one last time. He said it was okay, but he did have a deputy keep an eye on me.

The ground was all wet and muddy from the melted snow and firefighters' hoses, but I still found where me and Miz Simmons spread Lazarus's ashes all them weeks before. I bowed my head and let the tears come again. "I know you'da saved her if you been here," I told him. "You purely existed to give your life for hers. I promise you, if it takes all my days, I'm gonna get Junior Flint for this. And I'm gonna send him straight to Hell."

Then I got in the truck and drove on home.

2

Getting ahead of myself, I do that a lot when I look back on them days. The middle of the story becomes the start, and then I jump back and forth, trying to remember everything. Let me go back to the beginning, so you'll know how things went from there.

All this took place some ten years ago. The year I turned sixteen, a year full of death. Seemed like everybody I knew was dying. Well, not really, but three of my nearest and dearest was taken in a matter of months. Felt like I was too young to have to deal with that kinda misery. But deal with it I did.

First, Dad died in early summer. Made me grow up faster'n I wanted to. Somebody had to take over being the man of the family, and me being the oldest, it was up to me. Had to quit Lewiston High and give up my dream of how I wanted my life to be. Kept telling myself this must be God's plan, so get on with it.

Only right the West Virginia Coal Company paid for the funeral, him being killed when the shaft caved in. Everybody else got out, so it was just Dad left in there. Company give Mom something "for compensation." A pay-off we all thought, but what was she gonna do? Sue 'em? What with? How'd she pay a lawyer? So she took the money, and I went to work once we got through the funeral.

I used Dad's old truck to get round, bagging groceries down at the Busy Bee, washing cars at the PayLo Gas Station. But them two jobs together wasn't enough. Mom had five children to feed, and that pay-off wasn't gonna last for long. I needed me a real job, but I didn't see how I was gonna find one, 'cause I was too young. Didn't even have a high school diploma, so who was gonna hire me?

Then I heard about this widow come to live outside Lewiston on the old road to Morristown, the one nobody takes no more, 'cause it's too curvy. Rather use the Interstate. Gets 'em there faster and safer. Anyway, I heard from the manager of the PayLo that she was looking for somebody to help fix up this old cabin she bought. Dad was handier with tools than I'll ever be, but he taught us boys everything he could, and I figured I could hammer and saw with the best of 'em. So I drove out there one day, between bagging at the Busy Bee and washing cars. Hoping she'd see the advantage of hiring someone cheap 'cause they was young and eager.

I knew where that cabin was. Musta stood there two hunnerd years at least, always in the Thomasson family. Then Clyde Thomasson took it into his head to go work in some Cleveland plant. Nobody never seen him since, and the whole place fell to ruin.

I drove up over the ridge from Lewiston, past the old lumber road where they cut down all the hardwood years ago. Turned onto the dirt track that led down into the holler where they built that cabin, and the first thing I saw was the roof caved in. Not all of it, but bad enough it was gonna take some work to keep the rain out. Tree growing up through what was left of the porch. Most of the walls looked okay though. Thick, made of logs from trees so big you don't see 'em like that no more. Looked like chestnut, before the blight killed all their beauty. Them logs needed chinking, but I knew how to do that.

I parked the truck in front and couldn't see a window that wasn't busted out. Called out "Howdy" a bunch of times, but didn't seem to be a soul about. Door was off the hinges, so I peeked inside. Wasn't nobody to home. I could see where the rain come through the caved-in roof and made a mess. Them wide-planked, hand-hewn floorboards was covered in wet leaves, and the smell of rot and mildew was everywhere.

Sure was gonna be a lotta work, getting that old place back in shape. And that was a good thing for me, if not for the widow.

Then I looked round outside some. All I could see was destruction, from the tumble-down stone walls that marked the bottom land to the overgrown vegetable garden them Thomasson women musta tended for generations. The chimney looked pretty good, though, mortar just needing a little patching here and there between the fieldstones.

Still, it was a gloomy place, set under giant trees that cast deep shadows even though the sun was full out. A big log'd come down across the creek that run through the holler, like a footbridge made by God. Not much water in that creek, but it'd be full to gushing once a heavy storm come. The smell of rotten wood was all round, what with some of them old trees falling down and being left to lie in the moldy leaves. Hard to imagine why a woman'd ever wanna live alone in a place like that.

I started back to the truck and took a fall 'cause of a hole some critter'd dug. Fox, maybe. They do that if they smell something underground. I rolled over, looked in that hole and let out a gasp. There was bones down there, laying every which way. Fox musta done that. So I stirred 'em up myself, trying to figure out what was buried there. Didn't wanna think it was one of them Thomassons, even though people did bury their dead on the farm back in the old days. Finally decided maybe some Thomassons buried a dog. Them bones wasn't human, 'cause the hip was all wrong. It kinda give me the shivers, though, and I set off for the truck at a trot.

I found a scrap of paper laying on the dashboard and wrote to say I'd be glad to help. Signed my name and cell phone number and tucked it in the cabin door jamb. Then I drove back to the PayLo just in time to put on my coveralls and get to work.

Well, the widow called me that night and suggested we meet at the Quik Treet the next day. That's this drive-in, been here long before them fast food chains arrived, and I hope it'll be here long after they're gone. Food's a lot better, and you know you're dealing with somebody local. They got a few tables inside, and that's where she said we'd meet up.

I set down facing the door, and it wasn't long before this woman come in who didn't look like nobody from round Lewiston, and that's for sure. Looked like she lived in the city a long time and was trying to fit in but didn't have the hang of it yet. Jeans too new and big bucks, same for her shoes and handbag. Looked like money come to her easy, and she knew how to spend it. Even her hairdo was wrong, high-style like something you see on the TV.

She come right over and introduced herself, so she musta figured out who I was too. Anyway, I stood up and shook her hand.

She sure smelled nice. Not that drugstore perfume some of the girls at Lewiston High wear. Hers was differnt, sweet and spicy like them flowers we planted by our church door. Pinks, is that what they're called? Anyway, she smelled just like she looked, expensive and not from round here.

"Hi there," she said. "You must be Jimmy Lee. I'm Sarah

Simmons." Deep down, under the education that was plainly there, you could hear just the faintest memory of West Virginia in her voice. Where'd she come from? And what was she doing back here?

Miz Simmons looked me up and down, like she was measuring me for a suit I could never buy. I sure felt awkward, but I held my ground and tried to look her in the eye.

"How old are you?" she said, and I had to tell her my age. Woulda liked to ask hers but knew enough to keep my mouth shut. Guessed she was forty or so.

It give me a worry now she knew I was just a high school kid, but I wasn't gonna quit yet.

"I may be young," I said, "But I'm big and strong. And I know how to fix most things round a house. I ain't afraid of work, and I really need this job." My eyes got all blurry then, and she musta noticed, 'cause she suggested we get something to eat before we talked any more.

We went up to the counter, and she said she should pay 'cause I was doing her a favor to meet her there. Made me feel a little shamed she wouldn't let me pay my own way, but I tried to be as thoughtful of her feelings as she was of mine. We carried our Cokes and little red plastic baskets of burgers and fries back to the same table and set down.

She dipped a couple fries in the little paper tub of ketchup they come with, chewed 'em good and said, "So tell me why you need this job."

And the way she said it, like she really wanted to know, not just for herself but for me, that warm way of asking made me open up. I didn't feel pitiful no more, and I laid it all out for her. Dad dying in the mine, Mom not having enough to take care of everybody. Me being the man in the family now, and working two jobs wasn't going to fill our needs.

She didn't lay a wet blanket of sympathy on me. Didn't reach out a hand and stroke my arm with more comfort than I could bear. "Okay," she said. "Let's give it a try. You come out to the cabin everyday for a month. I'll pay you the same thing I'd pay a carpenter, and we'll see how it goes. If we find we suit each other, we'll carry on. If it's not working for either of us, we can walk away, no harm done. How's that sound?"

It sounded so good I couldn't hardly believe it. But I tried to be a man and said a month's trial seemed just the thing for both of us. Said it righteous, just like she did.

Now, looking back, it seems so easy, how I got on a road that led to misery and murder. Deepest misery of my life, worse'n when Dad died. You learn to accept that miners can die any day they work a shift. You know they live with danger, and you half-expect 'em dying anyway. It takes time, but you can get over it.

But when loved ones are taken from you without no rhyme or reason, that kills you too. You know you're supposed to accept God has a plan for you when terrible things happen. But that was a misery so bad, I nearly lost my mind.

3

WE SET TO WORK THE NEXT Day. I quit both my jobs, worked full-time for Miz Simmons and never looked back. She kept me on all summer and into the fall, first fixing up that cabin so she could move in and then getting everything inside and out just the way she wanted it.

Surprised me to see how handy she was, even had a tool belt. I tried to ask about that without seeming too nosy, and she said she was an engineer's daughter. He didn't have no sons, so he taught her all the stuff he woulda taught his boys, if he'd had any.

She was renting a furnished place in Lewiston, but she wanted to get moved in as soon as she could. That meant fixing the door and windows and roof first thing. We soon realized we needed another pair of hands for the roof job, so I got my cousin Mitch to come over. He was older'n me, somewhere in his twenties, big like me—all us Schumans are—and he was working as a carpenter over at Bradley Construction part-time, when they needed him. We got them new rafters and joists up in no time. Covered 'em with plywood and shingles and had that cabin snug and dry. Wasn't no way rain was gonna puddle on them old floorboards once we got done.

Took about a week, and we finished that roof round midday, so Miz Simmons give us a celebration under the sycamore tree out back of the cabin. She brought a new grill from Sears, and Mitch started cooking burgers and dogs to beat the band. She had me get the cooler outta her Chevy Suburban, and there was everything to make a perfect picnic. Potato salad with sweet pickles, coleslaw, sliced tomatoes and onions for the burgers, mustard and ketchup and relish. She even had chili for the hot dogs, and we heated that up in a little pan on the grill.

She was determined to move in that day, even though everything wasn't finished inside. Her big ol' SUV was full of stuff she needed— sleeping bag, air mattress, camp stove, pots and pans, food and water. I carried all that into the cabin while Mitch finished grilling. Checked the toilet one more time to make sure it was still working. There was a septic tank we were going to have to get cleaned out, but she'd be okay for a while.

Then we loaded up our paper plates and set down on some overturned logs. Her and Mitch had a beer, and I got ice tea, but that was okay by me. I'd be drinking beer soon enough. After we had our fill of all that food, she brought out this chocolate cake she made the night before. Felt just right to be setting there, the three of us, looking up at that new roof and talking about how she come to live in Lewiston.

Seems her husband died of cancer in Baltimore, had that kinda cancer that takes a body a long time to go, months and months maybe. Well, when he finally up and died, she decided she wanted the peaceful country life. But she didn't decide that right away. There's more to it than that.

Turned out she was raised right here in Lewiston. She went off to college and never looked back. Got a job in Baltimore, met the guy she was gonna marry and settled down. No kids though, they wasn't lucky that way. Still, they had a good life. Then her husband was gone, and naturally she started thinking about what she was gonna do next.

Well, she started turning her life into stories. That's how she made sense of it, and before long, her book sales was pretty good. But she still felt empty, as empty as that big ol' house in Baltimore. That's when she come to realize what she needed was a small house in the country. She needed to come back to her roots and build a new life.

I set there, listening to her tell the story of how she come to Lewiston and smelling the warm smell of summer, wildflowers in bloom and crushed grass where we walked on it. High up, a hawk was circling, looking for something to feed her chicks, and I thought how sad it was Miz Simmons didn't have nobody to care for no more.

She wasn't that old. Turned out she was fifty. Sure fooled me, I had her pegged at ten years younger. She had this honey-colored hair, just getting streaked with silver here and there, and she still kept her figure.

"You should get married," Mitch said and give her a wink. "A fine-looking woman like you." Mitch always was a flirt, even at church, where he should know better.

She coulda remarried was my guess, if she stayed in Baltimore and met some educated man. All the educated men round Lewiston was already married, and the uneducated ones'd be put off by Miz Simmons, her being a writer and all. Well, I only went to tenth grade, but I wasn't put off by her. She treated me like she cared. Made me wanna tell my story, but not with Mitch there. He'd only make fun of me wanting to be a preacher. But I just felt like she'd understand me having that dream, even if it couldn't come true.

The grill was smoking from a piece of burned burger. When Mitch said that about her getting married again, she got up and threw some water on the coals. That only made the smell worse, but I figured she didn't wanna answer such a stupid question.

That's when we heard this sound, kinda whimpering way off in the brush behind the cabin. Made my hair stand on end. I was wondering what we should do when Miz Simmons took off, passed the grill and headed up the holler. Mitch was right after her, so naturally I had to follow.

The whimpering stopped once we started crashing through the brush, and we had a hard time figuring out where it come from. But Miz Simmons wasn't gonna give up easy. She motioned for us to stay still, and she threw the piece of burned burger she grabbed off the grill out into the brush. I didn't even know she had it, but just goes to show how smart she was.

She motioned us to back off and kneel down behind some honeysuckle. Felt like we was there a long time, knees hurting and almost choking on that sweet smell, but nothing happening. I was getting fidgety when we heard something crawling toward that meat. From the sound of it, it wasn't real big, but it was big enough. At least it was still daylight, so it wasn't likely a wildcat. That give me some comfort.

We was peeking through the leaves of that honeysuckle, and finally we was rewarded for our patience. This dog come crawling through the brush, half on its side, grunting with the effort and whimpering with the pain. Looked like a wolf, big, mostly black with tan here and there round his face. He sure was hurt bad. I couldn't see what was wrong, but it was pretty clear he wasn't gonna jump up and hurt us none.

"You two stay here," Miz Simmons whispered, "and keep an eye on him." Then she scooted backward through the brush, making just about no noise at all. Me and Mitch watched the dog swallow that meat and then just lie there, panting like he was near his last breath. Before I knew it, Miz Simmons was back with an old army blanket and a length of rope. She made a big slip knot in the rope and told us to wait. Then she started toward the dog, as slow as a caterpillar, staying low and speaking in the softest voice I ever heard.

"Hey, boy. Good boy. Nobody's gonna hurt you. You're safe now. Quiet now, quiet. That's a boy."

Me and Mitch stayed where we was, watching and waiting. That dog just laid there, looking at her, the whites of its eyes showing and its legs quivering to move somewhere, anywhere. But he spent his last little bit of energy getting to that burned burger, and there wasn't no strength left to do more.

Miz Simmons started to slip the loop over his head, and then she stopped, like she couldn't figure out what to do. Something was the matter, but I couldn't see what was bothering her. Then she did the bravest thing. She laid a hand on that dog's body and stroked him like he was more precious than gold, all the while soothing him with that soft voice.

She pointed at the army blanket and motioned us to come forward. We tried to be as gentle in our movements as she been. Don't think we managed that very well, but we brought up the blanket, and then I saw what was wrong.

That dog had a loop of wire bit into his neck so deep some of the skin growed back round it. There was pus everywhere, the smell of rotten flesh and blood too, where it seemed like he managed to break the wire and set hisself free. No wonder Miz Simmons hadn't liked to put rope round his neck.

"We got to be as careful as we can," she said, stroking that poor dog's coat with one hand and motioning with the other for us to get round behind him. "Mitch, you put both arms under him and lift him up just enough for Jimmy Lee to slide the blanket under. Careful, now, we don't want to hurt him any more than we have to."

Well, I wasn't sure this was gonna work, and Mitch looked like he didn't believe it neither. For one thing, that dog was mostly German Shepherd, and you know how mean they can be. I could see every tooth in his mouth, where he was panting, and it seemed like each and every one of 'em could rip us to shreds.

"Come on, boys," Miz Simmons said. "He deserves our best." Well, we done what she asked, and soon that dog was wrapped up in the blanket so he couldn't hurt no one. Not even hisself, 'cause he couldn't struggle. Mitch picked him up, and the dog cried out, but he laid still in them strong arms. Miz Simmons led the way, and before long, we was back at the cabin.

She uncovered the dog's head just a bit and dribbled some water into his mouth. "Don't want to give him too much," she said, "The vet might want to put him to sleep before he cuts that wire out."

We loaded the dog into the back of her Chevy, drove into town and up to the nearest vet. Miz Simmons went in and come out with Doc Friedman. He give the dog one look and said, "Yep, gotta operate."

Doc Friedman motioned us to follow him inside. Mitch bent to lift the dog, and I found myself saying, "Can I carry him this time?" Miz Simmons nodded, and Mitch stepped back to let me be the man. Felt myself full of wonder at what was happening to make me wanna do that.

We went inside and up to the desk. Woman there said she was Miz Friedman and we had to fill out some forms before her husband set to work. She put fingers to keyboard and said, "What's the dog's name?"

Miz Simmons looked at me holding that heavy dog, and she give us the sweetest smile, like a beautiful idea just come to her. "Lazarus," she said.

4

COURSE I KNEW RIGHT AWAY what she meant. We was gonna bring that dog back from death's door, just like Jesus brought Lazarus forth from the tomb in John, Chapter 11.

Hope I'm not committing the sin of pride, but I know my Bible pretty good. Read it everyday when I wake up, before I even wash my face and brush my teeth. Starts me off right. Directs my mind to where it oughta be. Gives me guidance when I need it and comfort in my trials.

I go to the Church of the Holy Light, Pastor Bob Marvin's ministry in that converted warehouse just outside of town. It's not like the Baptist or the Methodist church, or any church you ever heard of. It's one of a kind, started by a righteous man who got the Call and started to preaching.

He preaches the simple life, and he practices what he preaches. Money you put in the collection plate goes for good causes, not into Pastor Bob's pocket to buy Cadillacs or fancy suits. He dresses just like the rest of us, even for Services. No fancy duds to say he's the preacher. He buys used trucks and drives 'em til they die. Back then, his truck was probably older'n Dad's.

I never knew no one could move me to the Lord like Pastor Bob, and that's the God's truth. You might think a man like that'd be tall and impressive with wavy hair and a beautiful voice. But Pastor Bob is kinda short and wiry. He's pretty bald now, but his hair was already thinning out then, and he was only in his late thirties. What hair he had was straight and sorta this mousy color. Even his voice, then and now, is just kinda average, not deep and booming. But when he gets to talking about the Lord, then you know he has the Call. Every ear in the church is tuned to his message, and that message never fails to bring us closer to heaven.

I thought maybe I got the Call too, and I talked with Pastor Bob about that. We was setting at his desk in his tiny office at the back of the church. Bright sunshine was shining through the windows like God's own light come to give us wisdom.

"You keep on living your life," Pastor Bob said. "Help your Mom and wait for all to be revealed. If that's God's plan for you, you'll know it when He's ready."

So that's what I done, helped Mom by helping Miz Simmons, trying to be the best son and brother and friend I could be. That's the way I saw myself, a friend to Miz Simmons when she needed one.

So anyway, she had Miz Friedman type in "Lazarus," and Lazarus he was 'til the day he died. Us three set out in the waiting room while Doc Friedman did his best, but the waiting went on and on. Finally Mitch said he had to be getting on home. Miz Simmons told me to take him to the cabin in her Chevy, so he could get his truck, then come back for her.

By the time I did that, she was in with Lazarus, and Miz Friedman told me to go in too. Down the hall I went, into a room full of sick animals in cages, dogs with broken legs, cats been spayed and God knows what other afflictions. Everything lit by fluorescent lights so bright they hurt your eyes, and your nose wrinkling with the smell of animal and disinfectant.

Found Miz Simmons with her hand through the bars of a big cage, stroking Lazarus's fur, even though he was still knocked out and couldn't know she was there. Or maybe he did, maybe he heard her soft voice and felt her touch and knew he been saved. It hurt me sore to see him like that. But also made me feel good, seeing her give him the love he maybe never had.

Doc Freidman come in, drying his hands on a bunch of paper towels, blood and pus from Lazarus still on his rubber apron. Said we might as well go home, 'cause the dog had to stay at least overnight, maybe more before he could leave. So Miz Simmons give Lazarus one more stroke and whispered something soft. She turned to go, and I snuck a hand between the bars to touch ol' Lazarus too. His fur felt all wet and matted after the operation, but I didn't mind that none. I wanted him to know at least two folks was gonna treat him kind.

Miz Simmons was looking all beat-down, so I said, "Why don't we go for a cuppa coffee before we hit the road?"

She give me a nod and drove to the Corner Cafe, not even saying a word. Guess she was too worried to talk, even with me.

Just when we got to the door, Hank Conner come out, and she stopped in her tracks. He give her the meanest look, and she turned her head away.

I didn't know what to make of it, 'cause she was the most polite of women, and everybody in Lewiston seemed to like her. Why would a banker and real estate investor, a man old enough to be her father, look at her that way? Did he wanna buy the Thomasson cabin, and she beat him to it? Or was it something happened while

Miz Simmons was growing up in Lewiston, before I was even born?

He pushed past her, this tall, skinny man. But it also seemed to me like he was shrunk someway, like a man who'd been big and tough once but was all shriveled now. He walked kinda bent over, like his back hurt him. I watched Conner step into his fancy car, Cadillac Escalade with a metallic green paint job. Then I looked at Miz Simmons, and she seemed like she been hit with a two-by-four, right in the stomach.

"What's the matter?" I said, but she just shook her head.

Then she pulled herself up. "I'm okay, good enough to drive. Let's go home."

So we skipped the coffee, and I was left to wondering what was going on. She didn't talk much on the way back to the cabin, but I didn't feel like it neither. She pulled up beside Dad's truck, and I patted her arm.

"Don't you worry none," I said. "Lazarus gonna be okay. Doc Friedman's right up there with the best of 'em."

She squeezed my hand and said. "I know, Jimmy Lee. We're all going to be just fine."

I was late getting to the cabin the next day, 'cause Mom had to take the baby to the Emergency Room. He was all colicky, and she tried everything she knew, so there was nothing to do but to set and wait her turn along with all the other folks too poor to go anywhere else. That meant I had to watch the rest of the kids. I called Miz Simmons, and she said not to worry. Doc Friedman told her Lazarus could leave, so she'd gone off to get him and wasn't to home anyway.

By the time I got to the cabin, she was driving up too. I helped her unload Lazarus from the back of her SUV. He was awake but kinda wobbly on his feet, so I got a piece of plywood and made a ramp for him to walk down. He had a big bandage round his neck and an even bigger plastic cone that stood up all round, so he couldn't get at the stitches with his claws and break 'em open. God only knows how much all that vet-care cost, what with Doc Friedman operating and them pills Miz Simmons had to give Lazarus everyday.

That dog had to be in pain, but he seemed to understand we was there to help. Miz Simmons went back to the car and got the blanket Lazarus been laying on. The same one me and Mitch used to carry him outta the woods. Wasn't too messed up from Lazarus's wounds, and his smell had to be on it. She put that ol' blanket on the porch, and Lazarus went over and laid down. He give out a big groan mixed with a sigh, his eyes shifting back and forth between me and her.

"That where he's gonna sleep?" I asked.

Miz Simmons allowed as how he was gonna sleep indoors, beside her air mattress. "Later on," she said, "when we move in my furniture, he'll sleep right beside the bed."

That kinda brought me up short, 'cause most folks I know don't let a dog inside. Dogs is for outdoors, where they guard the house, herd the sheep and keep the foxes away from the hen house. Or they're hunting dogs, bred to scent. Either way, them dogs don't belong inside the house. We had a collie mix in those days, and Butch never spent a day indoors in his life. Had his own house, out by the barn, with a worn-out quilt to sleep on.

But if that's what Miz Simmons wanted, I was gonna help. So I knocked some boards together to make him a low box, and she got her husband's old jacket from outta the house and put it inside his bed.

"We'll leave him out on the porch for now," she said. "But when we come in tonight, I'll bring the blanket too, so he'll know this is his place. Later on, when he feels more at home, I'll wash that blanket, but it's okay 'til then."

Course here in the hills and hollers of West Virginia, just about everybody's got a dog. Like us with ol' Butch. But I never seen one like Lazarus, before or since. I gotta admit, though, he was one sorry-looking animal for a long time. Sorry-acting too. Wouldn't let nobody touch his ears, not even with a gentle hand, not even Miz Simmons. And God forbid you come by with a broom or a shovel or anything that looked like a stick. He'd cringe like he knew he was gonna get beat. Somebody'd punished that dog again and again, picked him up by his tender ears, hit him with a stick. That much was clear as day.

Miz Simmons, she paid attention to all that. If Lazarus didn't want his ears touched, she let 'em be. But once the stitches was out, slowly, slowly, over a lotta days, she eased her hand up from his shoulder to his neck to the top of his head and then to his ears. All the time giving him a soft caress and her gentlest voice. Finally—it musta took a month or more—she got him so he realized that having your ears fondled is just about the nicest thing there is.

She not only had him sleep in the house, she give him free rein. Lazarus learned on his own how to hook a paw into the screen door and open it hisself. Then he'd sail in and plop down next to wherever she was, cooking in the kitchen, writing at her desk, reading by the fire.

There I go, getting ahead of myself again. Over the years, them Thomassons put up a bunch of cheap partitions all over that cabin. Cut it up into little bitty rooms you couldn't swing a hammer in. So the day after Miz Simmons brought Lazarus home, we started taking down them partitions and making the cabin one big room. Sofa and chairs and dining table at the front, kitchen next, then her bedroom and desk.

The bathroom was in a lean-to at the back, and we had to do a lotta work there. We got Joe Henderson to come clean out the septic tank not long after Miz Simmons moved in. She had the well water checked by some lab, and it was still good. We put in a new pump and installed all the new stuff she bought, toilet and shower and sink. Ended up with a pretty nice bathroom, even if it was real small.

The new kitchen had one cabinet just for Lazarus's food. No table scraps and bones for him, not like other folks done for their dogs. Lazarus had his own special food she bought down to Hardman's Feed Store, cans of meat and sacks of nuggets. Sure done him a world of good. Before you knew it, he was strong and healthy, his coat all shiny from the spoonful of oil she mixed with that food.

I don't know how no city woman could know as much about dogs as Miz Simmons did. That woman had some kinda magic. She trained Lazarus just how she wanted him to be, and she never hit him once. Just used her Mean Voice on him when he was bad. That's what I called it, her Mean Voice. She'd put her hands on her hips and talk to him like he was the worst thing she ever knew. It was like that dog could understand every word and move she made. He'd hang his head like he was so shamed he like to die. But he never did that thing again.

When she come to give him attention, she bent over with her arms spread out and down like a mother hawk coming in to feed her young. When he saw her do that, he knew he was in for some loving. And he got so every time she started toward him like that, he come forward to greet her his own self. Then they'd stand there, him leaning against her and her stroking him and telling him what a great dog he was. And he was too, once she got done teaching him what it was like to live without hate.

Course Lazarus was smart. He deserved some of the credit too. That dog worshipped the ground she walked on, followed her round, even laid awake by her bed when she had to nap 'cause she got headaches so bad she took medicine that knocked her out in the middle of the day. He wouldn't tolerate nobody else to come near her except me. She saved his life, and he seemed to beg for the chance to save hers.

5

WE SPENT MOST OF THE SUMMER fixing up Miz Simmons' property. Got the whole house rewired, and not just 'cause everything was old and even dangerous. She needed more electricity than the Thomassons. Like she put in a stacked washer and dryer. But we also strung up clotheslines so she could hang stuff out to dry. Mom did that too, but in winter she hung our wet laundry inside near the cast iron stove.

And course Miz Simmons had a computer and a printer, so she could write her books. She mostly lived a simple life, just like Pastor Bob preached. Cooked her own food, not steaks or fancy food, just plain ol' country cooking. Washed her own dishes too, no dishwasher in that house.

Miz Simmons didn't have no TV, though she did like her music. And Lazarus did too. When she played some of her CDs, seemed like he smiled along with her to hear them notes come outta that box.

When we hooked that thing up, I asked her, "What kinda music you like?"

"All kinds," she said and pointed at the big box of CDs.

I helped her put 'em on the shelf I made, and she sure spoke the truth. She had country and classical. Old-time rock 'n' roll. Broadway plays I never heard of and live concerts from Carnegie Hall. I learned more about music just handling them CDs than I ever thought of.

Once we got everything set up, she said, "What'd you like to hear first?"

"Tim McGraw," I said, "'Humble and Kind'." So she pulled out *Damn Country Music*, and we listened to his CD all the way through. Didn't do no work, just listened. That sure was a fine way to end a day.

Course she had to get in an electrician to rewire the house, and she had to have a certified plumber for all that kinda work. But the rest of it, me and her done ourselves, only having to call on Mitch now and then when we needed a couple more hands. We rebuilt the porch lots bigger and painted it a nice white all over, except for the floor and ceiling, which she wanted blue. Sky blue for the ceiling and dark blue for the floor. Painted the new door sky blue too, like a welcome from heaven.

The kitchen cupboards was just ordinary, from Sears, and we put 'em up ourselves. Most of the furniture she brought with her, some of it family things passed down through the generations. Like her bed, solid oak and four poster with quilts made long ago by the women in her family. But the rest of it was just basic, like her desk, an old table she bought at the Salvation Army.

We repaired all them rock walls the Thomassons musta put up years and years ago. Them four-foot walls was only round part of the flat land at the bottom of the holler. Miz Simmons also owned the banks that went up to the road on one side and halfway up the ridge on the other. The old vegetable garden been inside the walls, and we got that dug up and some sets planted the first year—onions and tomatoes, peppers and such. We planned a bigger garden for the next year, when we could start early and do it right.

Having Lazarus out and about during the day kept the deer and rabbits at a distance. But they managed to get in and eat some too. So that was something else we was gonna have to take care of when we had a full garden.

Miz Simmons wanted some flowers by the porch, so we went down to Rumbaugh's Nursery and got daisies for summer and mums for fall. We was gonna do more again next spring, when we could get seeds in early so the roots'd grow strong before frost come.

At the end of everyday, when our hard work was done, Miz Simmons brought out the ice tea and home-made cookies. Then she turned on some music with the windows open, and we set on them overturned logs we been using ever since that day when we celebrated getting the roof finished. We set there under the sycamore and talked over what we was gonna do the next day. The three of us setting there, me and her and Lazarus, that was about the most peaceful I felt in a long time. Lazarus and me, we was her family. Both of us beat up by life but not giving up, thanks to her taking us in.

It's not like things wasn't good at home. They was, as good as they could be. But a house full of children, a baby crying and Mom worrying over all the things she had to worry over, that wasn't exactly peaceful. Even though she was older, Miz Simmons seemed younger'n Mom. And she sure was happier. Full of plans for the future, while Mom was stewing about each and everyday. Course Mom was all worn down from having so many kids. And losing Dad just about done her in. Me too. But with the Lord's help, I could feel the pain of it starting to mend. And being part of Miz Simmons' family with Lazarus, that was a help too.

Well, once Lazarus was feeling like his old self, he took to running off when he got the scent of a bitch in heat. Only natural, but Miz Simmons couldn't have that. She didn't want him getting killed for attacking somebody who crossed him.

"No way I'm ever going to tie that dog up again," she said. "Let's build him a fence."

So we did, wood posts and sheep wire, 4-inch by 4-inch grid. Closed in all her land, right by the road and up the ridge on the other side of the holler. Seemed to me like more fence than was needed and musta cost a fortune. Why not just close in the bottom land? But that's what she wanted, so that's what we done. Used two runs of fence, one above the other, so it was eight feet high. That way, Lazarus couldn't jump over, and the deer couldn't jump in. Miz Simmons said the whole thing was worth it, and I figured now Lazarus had room to roam.

She bought a high metal gate and had the electrician hook it up so we both could use a remote to open and close it. Then, whether she was in house or car, she didn't have to get out and fiddle with the gate. And the whole thing, the fence and the electric gate, made me feel like she'd be safer if anybody ever got it into their head to cause some mischief round there.

Course Lazarus still barked and snarled when folks passed by, especially if they was on foot. But that didn't happen too often. The Flint brothers lived up the holler and over the ridge. They'd go squirrel-hunting and walk right along Miz Simmons' fence where it come partway up that ridge. They never trespassed, but them walking so close made Lazarus furious. Wasn't nothing he could do about it but run along side, bare his teeth and growl.

There was four of them brothers. Parents dead, so they shared the house they growed up in. Let it go to rack and ruin, 'cause every one of 'em was no-count. Flints'd lived up there since before the Civil War. Always marrying pretty close. All the men was big but not too bright. The youngest brother was a genuine half-wit, name of Floyd. Folks said his mother had him too late in life. Whatever it was, he purely wasn't right in the head.

Junior—that's the oldest brother—seemed like he always kept an eye on Floyd. If Junior was out and about, his half-wit brother was too. Junior protected Floyd from all comers. You know how some guys just love to bully anybody who's differnt. They only got to try it once with Floyd. Junior beat 'em up one side and down the other, and that was the end of that.

Junior was in his forties. Named for his pa, Josephus, so everybody called him Junior while his dad was alive. Guess the name just stuck even after the old man died. Or else Junior didn't wanna be called by Josephus, it being a strange name, even for someone like me, who studies the notes in his Bible.

There was a couple other brothers in their thirties, but they wasn't round much. Worked during the week in some plant over on the Ohio River and come home on weekends. They probably brought in the cash, while Junior and Floyd lived on welfare and whatever meat Junior could get with a gun. To be fair, Junior did work that farm some, but seemed like he didn't have much to show for it.

None of them brothers ever married. I figured no woman'd have 'em, or maybe they was too no-count to take on the responsibility of a wife and family. They all looked alike, tall and rangy with sandy hair and the kinda skin that burns as soon as you're five minutes out in the sun. Their faces and hands and arms and necks was permanently red.

But Junior was the tallest and the rangiest and the reddest. Good hunter too, won the turkey shoot every year. Had a child by that

Becky Phillips who never was any better'n she had to be. Dad said Junior was mean, the kinda boy who liked to pick up cats by their tails and whirl 'em round just so he could hear 'em scream. Oh, he never killed anything, Dad said, but he liked to see 'em hurt. I missed my Dad for lots of reasons, but one was him knowing the history of all the folks round about.

Junior drove the most wretched truck I ever did see. Looked like it been in a hunnerd wrecks. Banged-up black paint job with one red fender where he had an accident. Had to take whatever he could get down to the body shop with no money to pay for painting it to match. Scratches on the roof where he musta had a rack of lights some hunters use at night even though they're not supposed to. Probably put them lights on when he wanted to hunt and then took 'em off so nobody'd know.

Well, Junior'd drive by, Floyd hanging out the window waving and hollering for all he was worth. They didn't even have to be on foot for Lazarus to go crazy. He'd lunge at the fence like he wanted to jump through the truck window and tear somebody's throat out.

It wasn't that dog's fault he was the way he was. He been kept tied up for weeks and deviled within an inch of his life. And that'd make anybody mean.

On Sundays, our day of rest, Miz Simmons liked to roam the woods with Lazarus. She'd put him on one of them leashes that reels in and out so he could run, but he couldn't run off. She musta learned every path in them woods. Some of them trails is deep in the ground, go back to Indian times, but some of 'em is so faint, you almost can't see 'em, especially later in the year, when the leaves start to fall.

"How come you like to go on them walks?" I asked one Monday when we was sharing our Sunday news.

"I just like to commune with nature," she said. "Makes me feel closer to Creation." She smiled down at her dog. "Gives Lazarus some peace to be outside the fence. And lots of times, ideas come to me about what I'm writing. It's all good."

Well, better her than me, I thought. I went to church on Sundays, Bible Study at 9:00 and Services at 10:15. Felt the need of 'em both. Learning from Pastor Bob, hearing him preach, that was pure joy.

Course if I'm honest, there was another joy at the Church of the Holy Light. Eden Jones. She been a Pentecostal, but her and her momma started coming to our church, and her little brother went to the toddlers' nursery school.

She set next to me at Bible Study one day, and I couldn't help but notice how bright she was, inside and out. Like a new penny, come to grace my life. She didn't know her Bible as well as I did, but she asked questions that made us all think, Pastor Bob too.

I paid close attention to her after that, watching her shining eyes and swaying ponytail. Liked it even better when she wore her hair hanging down. Dark brown and just as shiny as her eyes. She had a nice figure too, though I shouldn't have been looking in church. One Sunday I worked up enough courage to talk to her at the Social the ladies have after Services. I sidled up to her at the coffee and tea table and said, "That sure was a good point you made. About why Moses and the Israelites had to wander so long in the wilderness?"

She smiled up at me. "Why thank you, Jimmy Lee."

Jimmy Lee? She knows my name? That got me flustered, but I was determined too. "You live round here?" Dumb question, I know, but I was thinking about offering her a ride home.

"Over at the Happy Hours Trailer Park. It's real close. That's one reason we started coming here. We can just walk back and forth."

Darn, I thought, that's not gonna work. "How about a piece of that coffee cake? Ain't no baker better'n Miz Stealey."

"I know," she said. "I always look for what she made."

That made me smile. "Looks like we got something in common. I sure do like my sweets."

And Lord help me, she smiled back. "Me too."

I just about hugged myself, 'cause I was thinking that was a pretty good start.

And it was too. That was the start of me and Eden coming to mean something to each other. She become part of my life, and I become part of hers.

6

LET ME COME BACK TO Miz Simmons going for walks with Lazarus every Sunday. They rambled all over them hills for hours on end. That's how she met Orrin Dent.

He had a pot field up on top of the ridge, on the opposite side of the holler from the Flints' place. Everybody knew it, but everybody looked the other way. And you never saw none of them police helicopters flying over. Somebody was on the take for sure.

Orrin'd drive his truck up this old lumber track and hide it in the bushes, so nobody could see. Not unless they walked right up to it. Then he'd hoof it up to his field deep in the woods. Dad said when he was a boy, nobody even knew what pot was. Now seems like everybody smokes it. Dad woulda skinned me alive if I did that, and I still ain't tried it. Even if he ain't here, I feel like Dad's watching over me, and I don't wanna let him down.

Anyway, Miz Simmons told me the whole story. Made it come alive, like one of her books. I should probably say here that I never read none of her books in them days. Truth to tell, I wasn't much of a reader, but it was more than that. I didn't feel like I needed to know her from her books 'cause I knew her direct, from being with her almost everyday. But that story of how she met Orrin Dent?

Even now, I can tell it myself, 'cause she told it so good, I felt like I was right there.

Miz Simmons and Lazarus come along one of them faint paths. Mid-summer, before the leaves begun to fall, so them two didn't make a sound. Before they knew it, they hit a clearing, and there was Orrin with a shotgun to his shoulder, saying, "Back off, Missus."

Lazarus lunged for him, and Orrin swung the shotgun, taking a bead right on his chest. Orrin wasn't much over thirty then, with long black hair tied in a ponytail. Short and hefty, like a fireplug. He don't like it, but that's what folks still call him, Fireplug Dent. Miz Simmons said he looked pretty scary, built strong like that and his shotgun at the ready.

She hit the button that kept the leash from reeling out and said, "Back, Lazarus. Now. Sit." Used her Command Voice that said, "I mean it and you better do it." And good ol' Lazarus, he knew what she wanted. He backed up and set down. Kept his ears up, though, watching and waiting.

Once Miz Simmons got Lazarus under control, she turned her attention to Orrin. "Sorry I surprised you. Is this your land? Didn't know you were up here." She held out her hand. "I'm Sarah Simmons. I bought the Thomasson place."

Orrin didn't take her hand and didn't lower the shotgun. "I know that. Everybody knows that."

She kept her eyes off the pot field and give him that sweet smile. "I don't care what you're doing up here. None of my business, and I don't want any trouble."

He looked at her a long time and said. "Me neither." He lowered the shotgun to point at the ground but still held it ready in case he needed it.

"You hungry?" she asked. "Got some homemade cookies in my pocket, enough for two."

He still seemed pretty suspicious, but he said, "What kinda cookies?"

"Peanut butter."

"Make 'em yourself, rich lady like you?"

"Not so rich, and I like to bake. Makes me feel like there's something coming out of the oven to reward my hard work."

He broke open the shotgun and rested it in the crook of his arm. Pulled a tin of Copenhagen outta his coveralls and said, "And what hard work would that be?"

"Fixing up the cabin and the land, trying to make that place my place."

Orrin put a pinch of snuff under his lip. "Working with Jimmy Lee Schuman. Bet he does all the work."

She smiled again. "Well, he does most of it, but I try to help where I can." Lazarus was getting fretful, so she put a hand down to calm him. "How about those cookies? Got anything we can drink with them?"

Orrin give her just the touch of a grin. "Got a six pack."

"Goes good with peanut butter," she said.

From that day forward, Miz Simmons took care to stay away from Orrin's pot field. Her and him got on good, even if Lazarus couldn't stand the man. Her motto was live and let live, but Lazarus still didn't get along with nobody but her and me. Everytime Orrin drove by, she waved, and Lazarus raised a ruckus. Orrin didn't like it much, even though he knew the fence kept him safe. He didn't want no dog calling attention to the fact that he was sneaking up to his field.

Every Sunday, while Miz Simmons was walking them hills and staying away from Orrin's pot, I was getting to know Eden better and better. One time, I suggested we go for ice cream after church. That was kinda dumb, and I knew it as soon as the words was outta my mouth. After church is dinner time, and besides, that was about the only hours I got to spend with Mom and my brothers and sisters. After me, Mom had four more, taking it in turns—sister, brother, sister, baby brother, all of us a few years apart. On the days I come home from helping Miz Simmons, I fell asleep after supper. I was that tired. But Sunday afternoon, the kids usually showed me what they done in Sunday School and how they was getting praise from their teachers. Told 'em Dad was proud of 'em, looking down from heaven.

But I did find a way to be with Eden. It was so simple, when it finally come to mind. I just up and offered to drive her to Lewiston High so she wouldn't have to ride the bus. She was taking algebra in summer school, so she could take an advanced course in the fall. She was real smart, lots smarter'n me, so most times I couldn't figure out what she saw in this ol' country boy.

But she musta seen something more'n just a ride. We both left home about the same time in the morning, and the Happy Hours Trailer Park wasn't that far outta my way, so picking her up wasn't no big deal. Them was some of the happiest times of my life, talking with Eden while we rode together every morning. Five days a week, and then I saw her on Sundays at church, so that meant I got to be with her almost everyday.

Orrin was just repeating gossip when he called Miz Simmons a rich lady. What with the fence and her getting famous as a writer and checks coming in at the post office, rumors got out she had a lot of money hid up there in her cabin. That was a bunch of hogwash, and I knew it. She kept her money in a bank down to Lewiston. Not Hank Conner's bank, though. Something going on between the two of 'em, but I still didn't know what. Anyway, some folks is ignorant, can't believe nobody'd keep their money in a bank.

And course the most ignorant of 'em all was Josephus Flint, Jr. Him with the two brothers who worked on the Ohio River and the other brother too slow to work at all. Junior kept worrying at that idea, that ol' widder woman—that's just about what everybody called her, at least behind her back—that ol' widder woman had money hid in her house. Junior talked about it all the time over to the Roadhouse. Get a couple too many beers in him and go on and on about all that money. At least that's what my cousin Mitch said. I was too young to go to the Roadhouse even if it was only for a beer.

I should probably say here and now that Pastor Bob wasn't like a lot of preachers. He didn't see no harm in a little bit of alcohol now and then. "After all," he said, "Our Lord turned water into wine," and I knew he was talking about that wonderful miracle in John, Chapter 2. Pastor Bob said the sin is drinking so much you're drunk all the time and take money away from your family. When I'm old enough to join Mitch at the Roadhouse, I'll have one beer—maybe two—and go home.

Well, back to Junior. Just like every other man round, he was afraid of Lazarus. So Junior bided his time 'til one day in July, when Miz Simmons took Lazarus down to the vet for some kinda shot. She was good that way, about the only person I ever knew to be so careful about making sure a dog had his shots.

Mom felt lucky when she could scrape together the money for her kids to get their shots before they started school. We sure never got shots for any of our dogs. Not when I was a boy, not when Dad was alive, and for sure not after he passed. Butch lived mostly on table scraps, slept in his doghouse in winter and died of old age. I dearly loved that ol' collie mix and took the best care of him I could. But Butch never had no shots.

Junior musta kept watch on the cabin pretty good. The road to Lewiston went round the top of the holler and down the other side of the ridge, past his house. So he probably saw Miz Simmons drive by with Lazarus in the back and knew his day had come. All he woulda had do was come cross the ridge on foot, cut through that eight-foot fence and break a window. And that's what he done.

But Miz Simmons didn't stay in town once Lazarus got his shots. She didn't wanna leave him alone in the SUV with all the aggravation of other people and dogs walking by. So soon as the vet was finished, she drove back home to leave Lazarus inside the fence.

She come up behind me when I was driving to the cabin to whack a bunch of that brush growed so thick we almost couldn't get through when we first found Lazarus. So we drove on together, and I was there for the next part.

Ol' Junior musta heard us coming and started to running. But Lazarus knew something was wrong and jumped outta the car window before Miz Simmons even stopped her SUV. He chased Junior all the way through that cut fence and took a big bite right outta the seat of his pants. Lazarus come home with that blue cotton in his mouth, just as proud as if it been a trophy. Guess it was, in a way. Miz Simmons laughed and praised him to the skies. And that Lazarus like to wave his tail so hard he took off like a helicopter.

But she didn't laugh when she got inside. Just about everything in that house was tore up. All our hard work gone to nothing. Cupboard doors pulled off the hinges, sofa and chairs and mattress slashed and the stuffing pulled out, even the table and desk upturned in case she'd taped something to their undersides. If it could be tore up, it was.

Wasn't nothing missing, though. Junior was looking for big money, not computers or CD players. They was both down on the ground, but they still worked. I know, 'cause I plugged in the CD player and put on Tim McGraw, just like that first day when she unpacked and we listened to "Humble and Kind."

I set to work trying to straighten things up as best I could, and Miz Simmons called the Sheriff. We was out in the country, so you called the county Sheriff, not the city police. Lewiston had a new police chief. The old one Eden and her friend Bethanne got sent to jail. They found out he was protecting somebody mixed up in all kinda evil, including the deaths of Eden's best friend and Bethanne's sister. That happened a couple of years before, and Eden told me all about it once we got to know each other. Didn't brag about it. That's not Eden's way. Just told it, like I told her some of my stories.

Anyway, Miz Simmons called Sheriff Price, and he took his own good time getting out to the cabin. We threw out everything that was ruined and had the place pretty well cleaned up by the time he arrived. Even had Miz Simmons' air mattress blown up, so she'd have something to sleep on 'til she could buy another regular one. I tried to tell her that it wasn't gonna do no good to call Jerry Price anyway. He was Junior's first cousin by marriage. Sure enough, Sheriff Price wanted to know if we got a good look at the intruder. That's what he called him, "the intruder." Well, course we had to say no, 'cause all we seen was the back of him with Lazarus not far behind.

Sheriff Price put a foot up on the rung of Miz Simmons' kitchen stool and said, "Then how you know it was Junior?"

I looked him right in the eye and give him the answer. "Cause that's all he talked about down to the Roadhouse."

"Talking's not doing," he said. So Miz Simmons showed him the piece of blue cloth outta the intruder's pants.

"Just common ol' work pants," the Sheriff said. "Every man in the county got at least one pair, buy 'em down at the Gmart for fifteen dollars." He paused, took off his cap and scratched his head. "Ma'am, I know this is important to you, but I got limited resources and too many troubles. People with a meth lab blowing up their house plus two car wrecks on these old country roads, and that's just today. I hope you understand, but I gotta focus on these life-and-death problems." Not long after, he drove off in a cloud of dust, talking on his radio and shaking his head.

Course he knew it was Junior broke in. Everybody knew that. All the men over to the Roadhouse had a good laugh at Junior's expense. Asked him if he bought any new pants lately, or could he recommend a pair with a tough seat. Wanted to know if he was gonna sign up to run the marathon down to the state capital next year. Junior answered 'em back, tried to give as good as he got, but Mitch said you could see he didn't like it none.

7

WELL, MIZ SIMMONS FIGURED IT wasn't worth the effort to contact the State Police. We didn't have no proof it was Junior, even if we was sure it was him. I had to agree, but it made me mad to think he was gonna get away with it.

She concentrated on getting her house back in order. Miz Simmons had insurance, and the check come pretty quick after she mailed in her claim with copies of all the receipts. Must be nice to have the money to buy insurance, I thought. Something like that happen to our house, we woulda had to do without 'til we got the cash to buy new stuff. I just prayed to God we never had to find out what it was like.

But the happy news about money was that having full-time work was causing me and Mom to feel things was gonna be all right. We been worried about keeping our little farm. Dad took out a mortgage a while back when my brother got real sick and had to stay on and on in the hospital 'cause of complications. West Virginia Coal Company health insurance didn't pay for everything, so Dad got a loan and put up the house as security. He'd almost paid off the whole thing when he died, so we didn't have many more payments to go. But we did let one slip after he passed. The man at the Lewiston Bank said he could understand we'd miss one what with the tragedy and just don't do it again. So we didn't. That was the first money outta my wages every month.

I do have to say, though, that if we been owing money at Hank Conner's bank, we probably wouldn't been treated so good. Remember Ananias in Acts, Chapter 5? Well, Hank Conner was just like that when it come to holding onto his money. Just as tight with his cashbox as he was uptight with his clothes. Always wore a tie, even when it was hot, jacket too. Button-down shirt and crease in his pants sharp as a razor. Man like that probably wouldn't wanna give Dad a mortgage in the first place.

Our house wasn't as old as Miz Simmons'. My grandaddy's grandaddy built our two-story wood house after the Civil War. Nothing fancy, but strong enough to last if we took care of it. And every generation done their best, keeping up the white paint on the outside and fixing whatever needed fixing on the inside.

Times was good when the house was built. Folks could live mostly off the land, just buying them few things they couldn't grow or raise. But times changed. A lotta sons didn't come back from World War I, so there wasn't enough men to work the land. Then the Depression hit, and my grandaddy had to sell off some land just to keep the family alive. Didn't get much for it, neither. Then World War II took his three oldest boys.

That meant Dad got everything. But he had to start working in the mine part-time to have cash money. Rest of the time, he practically run hisself into the ground, plowing and planting what land was left, keeping up what livestock we had. Mom and us kids helped where we could, especially with the vegetable garden and raising rabbits and chickens. We kept the same ol' bees been in our family forever, and Mom canned fruit from our trees and vegetables from our garden. All that meant we didn't have to buy much down at the Busy Bee.

But life sure seemed hand-to-mouth after Dad died. We had to sell the cow and calf early on, just to make ends meet. But I begun to thinking maybe we could buy new ones in the spring. That was the second thing outta my wages every month, putting a little bit aside so we could have us a cow and calf again.

After the break-in, I decided to keep an eye on Junior, and I asked Mitch to do the same. We both seen him all over the place, down to the feed store, out to the Roadhouse, on the road driving back and forth to Lewiston. Floyd always with him, stubble beard and scruffy hair hanging over his collar, dirty clothes and scuffed shoes. Junior mighta been looking after Floyd, but he sure wasn't keeping him neat and tidy. Course none of them Flint brothers was tidy to begin with, so maybe Junior never give it a thought. Like I say, we seen Junior everywhere, but we never seen him near Miz Simmons' place again. I reckoned he was being real careful after that.

The summer wore on, and me and Miz Simmons more'n once found tainted meat thrown over the fence. But Lazarus wouldn't touch it. She taught him never to take food unless it was from her hand or mine. Lazarus'd sniff at that meat and back off. If we wasn't there, he'd start to barking 'til one of us come to pick it up and throw it away. That was one smart dog.

One day in early August, Miz Simmons told me to take the next Tuesday off, 'cause she had to drive down to the state capital and take care of some business. She was gonna leave Lazarus with Doc

Friedman for safety's sake, so he wouldn't get deviled at home or in the city. Miz Simmons didn't say what business it was, and wasn't my place to ask. But the first thing that come into my head was maybe me and Eden could get together for more'n a ride. So the next morning when I was driving her to Lewiston High, I brought it up.

She give me this cute little smile. "You know how to swim, Jimmy Lee?"

"Sure do," I said. "Dad taught all us kids down at the swimming hole he made." That brought a lump to my throat, but I kept going. "What d'ya have in mind?"

"What if I skip school and we go swimming?"

My heart started beating so fast I couldn't hardly breathe. Skip school? Spend the whole day together? I been having physical feelings about Eden, even having some dreams at night that felt good at the time but bad the next morning. Made me feel guilty, having them dreams. Knew I'd never take advantage of Eden, respected her too much for that. But being together in swim suits? That was gonna take some strong willpower.

I was thinking about that swimming hole and how there wasn't nobody round to see. Too far from the house. The kids helped Mom all day and didn't go swimming 'til the afternoon. We could be gone by then.

I tried to talk, but my voice come out all squeaky. So I coughed like I swallowed something and tried again. "Where you thinking about going?"

She smiled. "Well, I usually go to the county pool. You ever been there?"

I swallowed hard again. "Nope. Always just go to our swimming hole."

"Well, its almost as free," she said, "and it's easy to get to."

Part of me felt relief, and the other part felt disappointment. "Okay," I managed to get out. "Whatta we do about changing? Wear our suits under our clothes?"

I could see she was trying not to smile. "No, they got dressing rooms."

So that's what we done the next Tuesday. Took our suits wrapped up in towels and changed in the dressing rooms. When Eden come out and I first saw her in a bathing suit, I thought I was gonna be embarrassed, my body reacted so strong. I managed to control myself, and we had a wonderful time. Had my arms round her more'n once, and that felt so good I still can't find the words for it.

On the way back to the Happy Hours Trailer Park, we stopped for ice cream at the Dairy Whip, setting there in the truck, talking and laughing and glad for the chance to be together. That's when I lost sight of my intentions. Before I knew it, I reached over, put my hand behind her neck, bent down and kissed her lips.

And she kissed me back. First-time kiss, and I saw my whole future before me. I was gonna marry Eden, raise our kids and live into old age, side by side.

8

ALL OF A SUDDEN, IT WAS September, and them wonderful days of summer, getting together so easy, was over. Eden was back in class all day, taking extra courses, studying hard to keep her grades up. I drove her to school a lotta the time, when it worked out for both of us, and we got together when we could. We was happy in each other's company, even if it was just setting together at church. We sure liked our kissing, but we was both careful not to let it go too far.

Later that fall, me and Miz Simmons was planting daffodil bulbs in the edge of the woods, over on the far side of the holler, away from the road. Up above us was the fence, halfway up the ridge, but we was still down in the bottom. It was beautiful out there that time of year. The night frosts'd turned all the trees to red and gold, like a sunset covered the hills with a patchwork quilt. I could hear the creek running strong with all the rain we'd had.

I was digging crooked little trenches, so the flowers'd look more natural when they come up. Then Miz Simmons crawled along in her old cords, put in a few bulbs here and there and covered 'em up with that rich black soil where the leaves fell and maybe never been moved for a hunnerd years.

Lazarus was laying there watching us when all at once he jumped up and took off like a shot. We could hear that ol' dog crashing through the brush I'd left higher up the holler. Miz Simmons called him, but he musta had the heat on him and couldn't pay no mind not even to her. He just kept on crashing through, getting farther and farther away. At first, we thought he was chasing some rabbit, or maybe a squirrel. We wasn't worried 'cause of that strong fence we built.

Then he started to growling, the way he did when somebody come to the gate. We both got up and looked through them red and gold leaves toward where the noise was. And we saw something bright blue moving fast, across the holler on the other side, where the road was. Lazarus was running after that bright blue, ears slicked back, fangs showing white against his dark fur. That dog was running for all he was worth. Out to protect Miz Simmons, I reckon.

Miz Simmons begun to running, and I run after her. She kept calling Lazarus's name, but it was like he was deef. And I was calling out to her, "Miz Simmons, Miz Simmons, you be careful now." I don't know what I was afraid of, that she'd fall, that Lazarus'd turn, that she'd catch that man in blue. Then I realized it was more'n one man. There was several bodies in blue up there. And they wasn't all together. They was spread out, the way you do when you're hunting wild hogs.

It seemed to take forever for us to get across the holler and start up the other side. Had to run to that big ol' downed log to cross the creek, then double back some. And all the way, Miz Simmons was calling Lazarus, and I was calling her. We could hear Lazarus growling and growling like he was gonna take on the whole world. Suddenly he yelped, a terrible yelp like to wrench my heart out, and I knew he was hurt awful bad. Had to be, crying out like that.

Miz Simmons looked back at me and run even harder. I couldn't bear for her to find that dog hurt, so I speeded up and passed her. Brush was beating against my face, and my breath was hurting deep inside my chest. I almost slipped and fell down the bank, but I put out my hand and caught a sapling at the very last second. That's all that kept me from falling twenty feet into that creek roaring with fall rains.

I found the place where they done it, where they caught Lazarus. You could see where he been thrashing. A lotta twigs was broke off bushes, and the ground was all tore up. But he wasn't there. No one was. Miz Simmons come up, breathing something hard, and we followed the trail of where they drug that brave ol' dog. At one point, we saw some blood on a leaf, but it was so high up, it couldn't been his. Lazarus musta bit one of them men and bit him good. They mighta had him, but he was putting up a good fight.

We followed that trail another twenty feet up to where it ended in a hole cut in the fence, right by the road. We climbed through and looked round, but wasn't nobody there. Just some tire tracks in the mud left over from the rain and the footprints of at least three men. And Lazarus's claws where he'd dug in and tried to stop 'em throwing him inside a truck. That's the kinda tire tracks it was, truck tires.

Miz Simmons started to running up the road, and I took after her again. I don't know how that woman was able to keep on running. I was young, but I was like to drop. We got round a curve, and there was Lazarus tied in the back of a pickup truck, jumping up as much as them ropes would let him, barking and tossing his head. Even from that distance, I could see it was a beat-up pickup, black with one red fender.

Just then, Orrin Dent come down outta the woods, rifle slung across his shoulder, two squirrels tied together and hanging over the barrel. "I seen what happened," he said. "I seen 'em load your dog into that truck. They gonna put his eye out." Orrin nodded his head and squinted. "Teach him a lesson he won't forget."

Miz Simmons looked back and forth from the vanishing truck to Orrin, her hands clutched to her breast. For the first time I ever knew her, it was like she didn't have no words to say what she needed. Her eyes roved back to the truck. It was rounding the next curve, and she musta seen that red fender too. Then she looked at me. Her face was full of pain and doubt, all mixed together like she couldn't trust her eyes and ears. One word slipped through her lips. She breathed it more'n said it. "Junior." Before I knew what was happening, she whirled round and down the bank along the outside of her fence.

I don't know why she didn't go back and get her SUV. She just took off through them woods like she knew exactly where she was going and how she was gonna get there. I run after her, keeping up best I could. She knew all the trails from them Sunday walks, even paths so dim I couldn't see 'em. Some of them trails wasn't no more'n a whisper through the woods. I don't think she considered her car for a second. It was like she was possessed or something, following a highway through the woods only she could see.

The Lord give us the luck, and I was thanking Him for it. Rain'd slid down and left them higher trails pretty dry. No slipping and sliding in the mud on the steep side of the ridge.

We got to the creek where the holler was rising between the two ridges. Crossed at a shallows Miz Simmons found without even looking. Started up the other ridge, and then we heard Lazarus let out a scream. That's the only thing I know to call it. That dog screamed like a woman in childbirth. I know, 'cause Mom bore all her children at home with only a midwife to help. That scream started off high and full of panic, then it just trailed down to a whimper. I hope never to hear anything like that again in all my life. It just pierced my soul.

I'll never know how we managed it, but we run faster, up over the ridge 'til we was on the edge of Junior's field. We could see across the dry, yellow grass to his old gray house. Probably never had a lick of paint in all the time his family lived on that ridge. And there was Junior, standing on the porch with two men, all of 'em laughing fit to bust. One of 'em was Junior's halfwit brother, Floyd, and the other was his cousin over to Valleyview-way. I knew him from sight, but not to speak to. Lazarus was laying at their feet, his back to us, his fur ruffling in the wind.

I looked round for something to protect us, a rock or a felled branch. I was worried maybe Junior had hunting dogs or guard dogs, and they'd come for us. But I couldn't find nothing to keep us safe, and I begun to feel scared about facing them three grown men and what they done to Lazarus.

Miz Simmons stopped running and drew in a long breath, like she needed all the strength she could get. She didn't look at me once. She just lifted her head and started forward, her step firm, her eye on her dog. And I took my cue from her. I squared my shoulders and marched beside her, step for step, eyes on Lazarus. We crossed that dried-up field, ready for whatever we would find.

What we found was Lazarus laying on his side, pinned to the porch. It's hard for me, even now, to say what they done. It hurts that bad just to remember. But that was the beginning of everything else that followed, so tell it I must. Them evil men, so evil I knew I couldn't never forgive 'em, they drove a quarter-inch spike in one of Lazarus's eyes, through his skull and out the other side right into the floorboards. His blood was smeared in a circle all round that spike where he'd tried to get away, but all he could do was go round and round 'til he died. Musta been what set 'em to laughing, seeing that poor, pitiful dog struggling round and round that spike in his own blood.

Junior stopped laughing and took off his baseball cap, so greasy you almost couldn't tell it been green once. "Why, Miz Simmons," he said, "how nice to see you. Looks like my ol' dog finally come home."

The men like to bust their guts laughing again. Floyd bent over, slapped his thigh and pointed to a broke-down wood fence. There, looped round one of the posts, was a piece of wire, its end snapped and laying in the dust. "Left that wire there," Junior said, "so's I'd remember him."

I couldn't bear to look at any of 'em. They was more animal than Lazarus ever thought about being. I went over to him and touched his coat. It was still shiny, like he only died a second before. There was this five-pound hammer laying upright against the step, kinda like a small sledge. I picked up that heavy hammer and swung upward with all my might against that spike, swung with all the grief that filled my body, all the memories I'd shared with that good woman and the dog who worshipped her. And I sent that spike flying across the porch and out into the field. Then I raised up Lazarus in my arms. He was limp and heavy, but I managed to hold on, get down the steps and across the bare yard.

My heart felt sore to break. I knew Sheriff Price still wasn't gonna do nothing, even though we found Lazarus like that on Junior's porch and them men laughing. Even though I probably freed him with the very hammer they used to drive the life outta him.

Then I saw Miz Simmons. She was standing perfectly still, staring at them men. It was like she was gathering all the power of the universe into her body. They stopped laughing and watched her. Junior's brother and cousin was shifting from foot to foot, but he was standing his ground, staring back with a smirk on his face. Slowly she raised an arm and pointed at their leader. Her voice was calm and quiet, like she was in church. "I curse you, Junior Flint, and all your family until the end of time."

The cousin from Valleyview fell back a step. Floyd went all the way in the house and peeked round the door jamb. But Junior kept on standing his ground and shouted back, "I ain't afraid of no widder woman and her boy-help!"

Miz Simmons didn't even bother to answer. She just laid her hand on Lazarus's side, and we walked like that outta Junior's land and down to the road that led by her house.

9

I KNEW I COULDN'T CARRY Lazarus all the way, but I didn't wanna leave him for fear of what Junior might do if he found him. We got down the road aways, and I was kinda staggering under his weight. Miz Simmons could see that.

"You go into the woods here and stay," she said. "I'll get the car and come back for you."

So that's what we done. I hid behind some blackberry bushes, afraid Junior was gonna show up any minute with a shotgun. Tried to keep the fear away by thinking about where we might bury Lazarus. But when Miz Simmons come back for us, we didn't drive to her cabin. Instead, she went into Lewiston to Doc Freidman and asked him how we could get Lazarus cremated.

I was just bowled over. I never heard of cremating no dog. Hardly never heard of cremating a person, 'cause if you do, how they gonna rise again when Judgement Day comes? Everybody I knew just buried their dogs deep and put a couple big rocks over 'em, so a fox couldn't dig 'em up. Like that skeleton I found when I first come out to Miz Simmons' place, before I met her at the Quik Treet. Doc Friedman said to leave Lazarus with him, and he'd see to it. He thought there was a way they could do that over to the University.

Miz Simmons was hopping mad, said she was gonna sic the Sheriff on Junior for sure, and if he didn't do nothing, she'd call the State Police. I said there was no point in calling Sheriff Price, 'cause he was kin to Junior. He'd find an excuse not to follow through, just like he done the last time she called him. Besides, Junior was mean and might come for her if she sicced the police on him.

Doc Friedman reminded her the State Police had their hands full with a prison breakout in the next county. No way they was gonna come over here for no dead dog even if his death been so horrible.

Our talking like that didn't calm down what she was feeling, but she seemed to understand calling any kinda cops wasn't gonna work. She just nodded her head, motioned me into the SUV and headed back to the cabin.

Well, somehow Doc Friedman managed to get Lazarus cremated, and a couple weeks later, Miz Simmons went down to the clinic to pick up his ashes. I went with her in her SUV, 'cause I didn't like to see her have to do that by herself. Then we drove back to her house, and she fixed us hot tea with the honey I give her from our bees before life hurt us so bad.

I carried the tray out to the sycamore, and she brought the cardboard box of Lazarus's ashes. We set there on our overturned logs and drunk our tea even though there was a cold wind blowing. Not talking. Didn't need to. When the tea was done, Miz Simmons put the tray and empty cups aside. Then she opened the box and spread Lazarus's ashes just where he liked to lay when all three of us was there in happier days.

I was supposed to be the man of my family, but tears was rolling down my cheeks. I looked over, and them same tears was on her cheeks too. We still didn't need no words, 'cause we both knew we lost our special friend.

Wasn't long before Junior started to get boils. Mitch said the first one just popped out in front of his very eyes one night over to the Roadhouse. A big red thing with a yellow head, right on the side of Junior's neck. Later, more come out, all over his neck and face. And down his back and arms. Halfwit Floyd told anybody'd listen that Junior couldn't sleep at night 'cause he had boils on his butt.

But that wasn't the end of it. Junior's teeth started to rot. First one, then the other. Rotted and fell right outta his head. But not before they taught him to live with pain day and night. Then Floyd was telling how nobody wanted to get near Junior 'cause his breath stunk so bad.

Well, course Junior got it into his head that it was all 'cause of Miz Simmons's curse that he was covered in boils and his teeth was falling out. Never went to no doctor. And sure never went to no dentist neither. Just used Becky's home remedies, and any fool coulda told him Becky Phillips didn't know nothing about curing no boils. Nor toothache neither. The only thing she knew about don't bear telling in polite company.

The men over to the Roadhouse had a field day telling Junior he was right, that ol' widder woman put a hant on him 'cause of what he done to her dog. And what was he gonna do about it? Mitch said Junior stopped coming to the Roadhouse for a beer every night. He was doing his drinking at home, buying whiskey from his cousin's still. And sacks of pot from Orrin too.

Them boils and rotten teeth was what I was thinking about that early November day when the fire took Miz Simmons' life. That dreadful day I needed the comfort of Eden's arms. The day I knelt down by Lazarus's ashes and swore a solemn oath. From that day forward, I was gonna get Junior Flint for killing the woman who saw me and Lazarus was lost. And give us both a home in her heart.

I suspected Junior couldn't take it no more, the pain, the men sassing. Heard Becky told him not to come round 'til he got hisself right. Deep down, I knew Junior come over the ridge like that time Lazarus took the seat outta his pants. Only this time, he burned Miz Simmons' cabin right down to the ground and her with it.

Didn't matter whether he knew she was there or not. Later on, Sheriff Price found out she took her SUV into the shop for repairs, and the garage man give her a lift 'cause she had the headache so bad. Maybe Junior saw her car was gone, maybe he didn't. Maybe he peeked in the window and saw her asleep, maybe he didn't.

None of that mattered. Junior killed Miz Simmons, and I was gonna get the proof or die trying. The only thing that give me any relief from that deadly sorrow was the thought Miz Simmons musta been knocked out by the strong medicine she took. I had to think that, so she didn't suffer none.

Her lawyer, name of Farnsworth, put notices in the West Virginia and Baltimore papers, but seemed like there wasn't no kin to answer. What was left of her body was down to the state capital for an autopsy, and it wasn't coming back. There wasn't gonna be no funeral. Hardly nobody knew her, not like I did anyway.

Decided it was up to me to do something. So some days after the fire, when I felt like I could stand it, I drove out to where the cabin used to be. The electricity was off after the fire, and Sheriff Price had padlocked the gate and put that yellow crime scene tape up. But that didn't stop me none. Parked the car outside the gate and climbed over. The early snow was all melted, and I could see muddy tracks where everybody worked to put the fire out. Some of them tracks was no doubt mine, but I had no desire to walk in them prints ever again.

I forced myself to go inside what been her home sweet home. Wading through ashes, smell of death all round me, I thought my stomach would turn. My feet stirred up little whirlwinds, and the real wind spun 'em away.

I looked at where the bed woulda been and figured some of them ashes had to been her. I gathered up a bunch of 'em in the old coffee can I brought from home. Went out and spread them ashes under our sycamore tree, along side of where Lazarus was. Didn't have no hot tea, but that was okay. I didn't need none.

It was raining the next day, one of them cold winter rains that eats into you so deep you think you'll never get warm again. Seemed only right, 'cause I been feeling cold inside ever since I spread Miz Simmons' ashes. Sheriff Price called and asked me to come in the following Monday at eleven o'clock and make my official statement. That only added to the frost filling my body and soul.

Spent the whole rainy weekend like that, full of freezing loss. Sure needed church when Sunday come round. Saw Mitch walking in with his sister's family, but I only waved across the parking lot. Just didn't feel like talking.

Eden seemed to understand what I was feeling. She set beside me in Bible Study and laid a gentle hand on my arm. Just letting me know I wasn't alone. Eden and Mom never met Miz Simmons, but they knew how she saved our family by giving me a job. And they knew how I cared for her. But they wasn't jealous, 'cause they each felt safe in the love I showed 'em even then, when I was hurting so bad.

Pastor Bob preached about Satan taking over people so all they wanted to do was evil. He asked us to pray for Miz Simmons' soul, even though she never come to our church and almost nobody knew her. And then he asked the congregation to pray for one who did know her, who worked along side her, and who was suffering a deep loss. I felt all eyes turn to me, and for a moment, I felt empty, like I wanted to hide. But then I felt the warmth of all that Christian love wash over me. The love I give to others was coming back to me. Not just Eden and Mom and our family, but everybody in that church was sending me the blessing I needed. When we went to the Social after Services, I went up to everyone in the room and shook their hands, even the littlest kids'.

I had no idea what to do now I didn't have work no more. That meant me and Mom was losing money everyday, money we had to have. So Monday, on the way to the Sheriff's, I drove through that same ol' winter rain to PayLo. Wanted to see if I could get my old job back. Owner said not so many cars getting washed in winter and to come back in the spring. He said sixteen year-olds was allowed to load and unload supply trucks and suggested I go by the West Virginia Coal Company to see if they had work for me. I confess I couldn't face up to begging for a job from the company that killed Dad. Well, they didn't really kill him, but you know what I mean. Decided to put that on the back burner until there wasn't no hope left. Mitch come in to buy gas just as I was leaving. He said there wasn't much construction work going on neither but he'd see what he could do.

All that made me real down in the mouth by the time I got to the Sheriff's. Had to wait a while in the hallway, but his secretary brought me a cup of coffee. I put in two sugars, drank it down and was feeling a little better when I got called into the office right after.

"Thanks for coming in," the Sheriff said, not bothering to get up. "Have a seat. Mind if I turn on a tape recorder to help my old memory?"

"Okay by me," I said and set down in one of the two wood chairs in front of his desk. Them chairs was all scratched, and the varnish was coming off where too many backsides been. But his metal desk looked all shiny and new.

He got right down to it. "So who you think hated Miz Simmons enough to kill her?"

My heart give a little jump. Here was the start of keeping my vow. "Junior Flint," I said. "He broke into her place and tore it up, he killed her dog, and he blamed her for all his troubles after that."

Sheriff lit up a cigar and leaned back. "Heard about the dog. You got proof of any of that, Jimmy Lee?"

"No sir," I said, "but I'm fixing to get it."

He set up and put his elbows on the desk. "You leave that to me and my deputies. I don't want you running around, upsetting the apple cart. If there's proof, we'll find it."

I wasn't ready to believe that, the Sheriff being related to Junior by marriage, but I held my tongue.

He leaned back again. "Anybody else you think had something to gain?"

There he goes, I thought, trying to pin it on somebody else. I just shook my head.

Then his body rushed forward and leaned across the desk. "What about you, Jimmy Lee?"

"Me?" My voice come out all squeaky, like them early days with Eden. Felt like a woodpecker was hammering inside my chest. "What I got to gain? She was like family to me, always treated me good. Losing her was like losing Dad." That last part come out like I didn't have no breath left to talk.

Sheriff Price knocked the ashes off his cigar into this big glass ashtray with some kinda emblem on it. "Farnsworth says she left everything to you."

I couldn't gather my thoughts. They was all scattered like they was running every which way. "Farnsworth?" I said. "What d'ya mean?"

"I asked her lawyer about her will. You get it all, Jimmy Lee. That's one helluva good motive." He grinned but not like he thought it was something funny. "Better'n Junior's."

I jumped up so fast I knocked over the chair. "But that's crazy. I didn't know nothing about no will. How could I?"

The Sheriff stood up. "That's what we aim to find out. She tell you?"

Felt like I couldn't breathe. "No! God's truth, I didn't know. I swear."

He smiled, this awful smile that said he had a lot to go on. "You was first on the scene, called 9-1-1. How we know you didn't set that fire, wait 'til it was going good and then call for help? Damn good coverup, if you did."

I lost all feeling in my legs, grabbed the back of the other chair and set down. "I come over the ridge from town, I smelled the smoke, I found the cabin on fire, and I called 9-1-1. I told the truth then, and I'm telling the truth now."

Sheriff Price set back down, and we went on for a while like that, him accusing and me denying. The whole time, that tape recorder was spinning round and round, taking down every word. But I stuck to it. I was telling the truth, and I knew the Lord was on my side.

Finally the Sheriff said, "I don't have any proof. But you're still the number one suspect. Maybe I can't use this tape in court, but I'm going to listen to it again and again just to make sure I remember every word you said." He stubbed out his cigar. "Don't even think about leaving town, 'cause I'll be on you in a heartbeat."

I stumbled outta his office, across the hall and down the steps. Felt like I was gonna puke, and I asked the Lord to give me strength and courage. Managed to get in the truck and laid my head down on the steering wheel. I was shaking so bad, I didn't dare try to drive. Sheriff Price thought I done it. Now I had to get Junior for sure.

10

IT WAS JUST LIKE PSALM 28 SAYS. "The Lord is my strength and my shield; my heart trusted in Him, and I am helped." Before the day was over, I felt Him holding me up.

I should probably say here that even though Pastor Bob and everybody I know used the Modern English Version of the Bible, I study the King James one my Grammy give me when I was baptized. It's not just that she give it to me. I like the poetry of King James. Feels more holy, somehow, like the language we oughta use with the Lord. Even though I couldn't talk like that to save my soul.

Wasn't long before my head was up off of that steering wheel, and I was driving through the pouring rain to Paster Bob. Knew I needed the wisdom of his faith and his life. I had the worries so bad I bust through his door without knocking, but he had the grace to offer me a seat in one of the wood armchairs a church member donated in memory of his mother. Them's real nice chairs, and they got padded cushions the man's wife made. Anyway, Pastor Bob give me a cup of sweet tea from the thermos on his desk. That helped almost as much as the calm of his presence.

I was talking a mile a minute, getting more and more upset, trying to tell him all that happened down to the Sheriff's office.

Pastor Bob let me get it all out. Then he put his hands across the desk and said, "Before we go any further, let's pray."

I leaned over, put my hands in his, and felt a heavenly peace as we prayed together, "Our Father in heaven, hallowed be Your name..." We got to the "Amen," and then Pastor Bob prayed just for me. I don't remember all the words he said, but he asked the Lord to show us the way forward in my hour of need.

And He did. Pastor Bob asked me to go back over some of the main points Sheriff Price had against me. Then he said, "Well, the first thing we got to do is go see Mr. Farnsworth."

Pastor Bob called up the lawyer's office, and Mr. Farnsworth said to come right over. So Pastor Bob put on his old baseball cap, and we climbed into his truck and took off. I was grateful he was driving and not me. Despite the peace that come over me when we was praying, I was starting to feel the willies in my stomach again. Besides, it was raining even harder, and I just didn't wanna deal with it.

We climbed the steps to Mr. Farnsworth's office, and his secretary showed us right in. Miz Simmons' lawyer got up to shake us both by the hand, and that impressed me. A man with that much education getting up and walking round his desk to greet us. Showed he was a man of character, made me feel like I could trust him.

He motioned us to sit down in a couple of soft armchairs and went back to his desk chair. "Now tell me how I can help."

"We've come about Mrs. Simmons' will," Pastor Bob said. "Sheriff Price says it gives Jimmy Lee a powerful motive to kill her."

Mr. Farnsworth wiped a hand down his mouth and chin and looked at me. "You're James Leland Schuman?" I nodded. "I owe you an apology," he said. "I was planning to contact you later today and ask you to come in, so I could read you the will."

"That's okay," I managed to say. "You can read it to me now."

He rummaged through some files and brought out a light blue one with a few pages attached. "James," he said, "the bottom line is that Mrs. Simmons left everything to you. Property, bank account and royalties with the right to pass these on as you see fit."

Felt like I was gonna choke. Only thing come outta my mouth was "You can call me Jimmy Lee. Everybody else does." Pretty dumb thing to say, but that's all I could think of. Them two men let me set there 'til I could get out my next thought. "Everything?"

"Yes," Mr. Farnsworth said. "Everything."

I was just dumbstruck. I couldn't take it all in. Miz Simmons cared for me that much? I been a good friend to her, and she didn't have no kin, but everything? Why didn't she tell me? So I asked Mr. Farnsworth that.

He smiled. "She wanted it to be a secret. She didn't want you to know. She felt death wouldn't come for years, and she didn't want you to be bothered about all that wealth while you were still a teenager."

"All that wealth?" Pastor Bob said. "How much are we talking about?"

"I haven't had time to evaluate everything," Mr. Farnsworth said, "but it'll be a couple hundred thousand at least. Probably more."

"Lord a mercy." That's all I could say, thinking how Mom suffered all her life without enough money to take care of the basics. Now I was gonna be able to help her and my brothers and sisters. Life was gonna be safe.

"I'm afraid we'll have to wait a year or more for probate," Mr. Farnsworth said. "But if you need cash, I could loan you some on the strength of the bequest in Mrs. Simmons will. Your mother would have to co-sign."

I wasn't sure what that meant, so I just nodded and looked at Pastor Bob. I was still having trouble wrapping my head round getting a loan. I wouldn't have to unload no supply trucks for the West Virginia Coal Company. But this lawyer didn't even know me. Why would he give me a loan?

Pastor Bob seemed to pick up on my confusion. "Jimmy Lee, do you understand what your mother co-signing means? Maybe we should ask Mr. Farnsworth to go over that with us."

God bless Pastor Bob. "Yessir," I said. "That's probably a good idea."

Mr. Farnsworth smiled with his eyes and said, "Thank you, Pastor Marvin. Should have thought of that myself. You're not old enough to legally receive a loan, Jimmy Lee. So your mother would sign for it also. Just a promissory note, showing what we agreed."

Pastor Bob nodded his head. "And Mrs. Schuman would have to put up the farm as security for the loan in case something went wrong. Isn't that right?"

Mr. Farnsworth leaned back and smiled. "Not necessary. I know you're good for it. We'll just write that when you get your inheritance, you'll pay off the loan first thing. If something goes wrong before probate, I'd still get paid from the estate."

If something goes wrong? That meant something like me going to jail for killing Miz Simmons like the Sheriff thought I done. I wouldn't get nothing then. For sure I had to prove Junior done it. I sure needed to think all this through and maybe talk to Pastor Bob some more. So I said I wanted to talk it over with Mom. Then I'd get back to Mr. Farnsworth about what we decided. They both understood, and Pastor Bob come back to the reason we come in the first place.

"When was the will written?" he asked Mr. Farnsworth.

"Last September, when her dog was killed."

Pastor Bob shook his head and looked up to heaven. "Maybe the loss caused her to contemplate her own end."

"I was there," I said. "I was there when Junior Flint killed her dog. I carried Lazarus home, and we spread his ashes under the sycamore where we all used to sit."

Pastor Bob put a hand on my shoulder. "Maybe the Lord worked through your act of kindness. You shared in her loss. Maybe that helped her see you were as much a son to her as one she might have borne."

"We can't really know her motivation," Mr. Farnsworth said, "but we do know she wanted you to be her sole heir."

"Can you tell Sheriff Price that?" Pastor Bob said. "Tell him Miz Simmons didn't want Jimmy Lee to know the contents of her will? Sheriff's got it into his head this selfless young man killed her to get his hands on her money."

Once we got outta Mr. Farnsworth's office and Pastor Bob took me back to get Dad's truck, the only thing I could think of was I needed to be with Mom. So I drove on home. All the while my mind was filled with a million questions. Mr. Farnsworth'd promised to see the Sheriff. But would Jerry Price believe Miz Simmons' lawyer about her wanting to keep her will a secret? Would something happen so we wouldn't get the loan to tide us over? What was I gonna do with all that land and all that money?

When I got home, the kids was still at school, and the baby was down for a nap. So me and Mom got to have us a good talk, setting at the table. Only table we had, in the kitchen. I told her the whole story, 'cause you can't keep nothing back from Mom. She can see straight through to the heart of you and tell you what you don't wanna say.

Mom being Mom, the first thing she said wasn't about the money but about trouble. "You think the Sheriff'll back off now?"

"Dunno, but I reckon I'll find out soon enough. Let's not worry about that now. Let's think about us getting the loan and letting go of the fret about me not having a job no more. Mr. Farnsworth says you have to co-sign the note 'cause I'm not old enough. He's gonna have me sign too, but I think that's just 'cause he wants me to feel like I'm part of the deal."

So we talked about signing a note to a man we didn't really know. Well, we did know Mr. Farnsworth had a good reputation round town, and we kept coming back to Miz Simmons' will and how he was gonna get paid regardless of what happened. Finally, we decided we didn't need to talk with Pastor Bob, we understood everything, and it seemed like this loan was the best chance for us to have a safe future. At least for now.

"Sure would be nice, Jimmy Lee, having enough money for the things we need. I'm not talking about the Wants. We never had the Wants. Too weighed down by the Needs."

"Okay, let's make a list of what we need. It'll keep our minds off the worries."

So we did—a warm coat for my little brother, shoes for both sisters, getting the fridge repaired 'cause I couldn't figure out what was wrong and winter booties for the baby.

"What d'you need, Mom?"

"Nothing, I don't need nothing."

"Mom, " I said with a soft voice, kinda like the one Miz Simmons used with Lazarus when she was coaxing him to do something, "you probably need more'n any of us. You're always putting everybody else first."

She shook her head and set there with her arms crossed over her chest, lips all tight and eyes out the window. I looked at her in her faded cotton dress and ravelly sweater, her shoes so worn they'd never take a polish, with Dad's old wool socks pulled up as far as they'd go.

"How about some new clothes?" I said. "Something warm for winter."

"Don't need no new clothes. Spend the money on yourself, Jimmy Lee. We ain't put nothing down for you."

"I'm fine, Mom. Really I am. I bought new work clothes when I got the job with Miz Simmons."

We set there, each of us stubborn as the other one. Finally, I looked up the stairs to the bedroom she shared with Dad all them years. "You ain't got Dad to keep you warm now. I'm gonna go down to the Gmart and buy you one of them fluffy comforters."

"James Leland," she said, her jaw clenched as tight as it could be and still let her talk, "I don't need no comforter. I'm gonna sleep under that blanket your Dad bought when we was first married. Sleep under it 'til my dying day, and that's all there is to it."

I give her a little smile, got up and went over to put my arms round her, bending so low I could smell the harsh store-brand soap she used to do the washing. "I hear you, Mom."

But I was gonna buy her that comforter just as soon as I got the money and tell her it was a Christmas present. She could still sleep under that blanket, just put the comforter on top.

Talking with Mom and Mr. Farnsworth, knowing we was likely gonna be able to buy what we needed, that was the Lord giving me the strength Psalm 28 talks about. I slept all through a long and peaceful night. But next morning, I was feeling the frets again, wondering if Sheriff Price was still gonna see me as his number one suspect.

I had to prove that Junior done it, but how was I gonna do that? First thing that come to mind was Eden. She had to deal with death and destruction a while back when her best friend was killed, and she helped send the bad guy to jail. I wasn't gonna let her get involved, but I sure could use her advice.

Told Mom I had a bunch of errands to run and took off for the Happy Hours Trailer Park. Realized I hadn't called ahead, but I was hoping everything would work out to talk with Eden. By the grace of God, the rain had finally stopped, but the whole world looked as bedraggled as I felt.

Eden come outta her trailer, looking both surprised and happy to see me. Soon as she got in the truck, she could tell I was sore afflicted, and she asked what was wrong. On the way to Lewiston High, I told her all about it. She just set there listening, now and then asking a question to make sure she understood. But she let me get it all out before she said, "Jimmy Lee, this is a lot worse'n what I went through with the Gravesly family. That family was a mess, and terrible things happened. But none of 'em as evil as burning somebody to death. We're gonna have to be real careful."

"No 'we' to it," I said. "I want your advice, but I ain't letting you lift a finger to put that devil in jail."

She set there, looking out the windshield. I drove up to the high school grounds and pulled over to let her out. Eden just set there some more. I begun to shift back and forth in my seat, and then she said. "Okay. Come get me after school, and we'll talk. Can you do that?"

I nodded, and she was out the door before I could say another word.

11

THE NEXT THING I NEEDED to do was tell Mr. Farnsworth what we decided, so I put the truck in gear and headed on over to his second-floor office. I was already through the door when I realized I didn't have no appointment. I looked across the room at his secretary. "Suzy Monroe," said the nameplate on her desk, "Notary Public."

"Scuse me, Miz Monroe," I said, "I was here yesterday with Pastor Bob Marvin?" She nodded like she remembered, and I went on. "Could you set me up with an appointment to see Mr. Farnsworth sometime today? I know it's short notice, but I need to tell him me and Mom decided to take him up on his kind offer."

Miz Monroe give me a big smile. "I was just getting ready to call you. Mr. Farnsworth drafted the note in case that's what you decided. It's in the computer, and we can easily make any changes you want. I was going to ask you to return tomorrow, but let me see if he has any time to see you both later today."

She looked through the daily schedule in her computer and said to come at 2:00, so I thanked her kindly and went back downstairs to the truck. I called Mom and told her the note was ready to sign at the lawyer's office and I'd come pick her up at 1:30.

Decided to use the time before then to take the list me and Mom made and go over to Gmart. Couldn't buy nothing at that point, but I could at least look at what they got. First thing I done was get me a cup of coffee at the snack bar and study that list. Didn't know any of the right sizes for the kids, but Mom could help with that once the day come to buy.

Had me a fine time wandering through the kids' section, looking at clothes and shoes. Gmart's got a lotta nice stuff, lotta styles and colors. I figured we could find just the right thing for everybody on the list, and I was looking forward to bringing Mom and making it happen.

That put me in mind of a comforter for her, so I went over to the bedding section and saw more comforters than I knew what to do with. Would she like a plain one or one with flowers or some other design? A clerk was putting things on the shelf, and I asked her if she had any ideas about that sorta thing. She asked did I want one that could be washed or had to be dry cleaned. Well, I didn't think about that. We never took nothing to no dry cleaner. Costs too much. But that wouldn't matter once we had us some money. Anyway, I didn't have to decide right then. Told her I was just looking, getting ideas for Christmas and wandered off to the automotive section to look at seat covers for Dad's old truck.

Before I knew it, it was lunchtime. Didn't want to bother Mom when she was getting ready to come to town, so I got a hot dog at the snack bar, along with some chips and a Coke. Left me feeling a little hungry, but I knew better'n to spend my money before it was in my pocket. Didn't know how long the money we had was gonna last, so best be careful 'til we got the loan.

Knew I was right to eat at the snack bar when I picked up Mom. She had on her best dress, the navy blue one she wore to church on special occasions, and she was carrying her good handbag. "Your sure look nice, Mom," I said. She gazed straight ahead out the windshield, but I could tell she was smiling.

Soon as we got to Mr. Farnsworth office, Miz Monroe showed us right in. Once again, he come round his desk to take my hand. "Glad we could get together as soon as the promissory note was ready." He held out his hand to Mom. "And I'm especially happy to meet you, Mrs. Schuman. You've raised a fine boy. That's what Mrs. Simmons thought, and I can see she was right to leave everything to Jimmy Lee."

Mom looked pleased out of all saying to hear that. She smiled real big and shook his hand right back.

He motioned us to sit in his soft armchairs. Both of 'em was covered in this heavy material with little shields like a knight might carry. I hadn't noticed that before. Been too shook up from what Sheriff Price said. Outta the corner of my eye, I saw Mom rub her hand on the material of her chair arm. Just feeling the quality of it, seemed like.

Mr. Farnsworth went round his desk and set in his own chair. There was a thin folder setting on the desk right in front of him. "Before we get to signing the note, let me bring you up-to-date on the Sheriff. I called and told him Mrs. Simmons didn't want you to know the terms of her will."

I was feeling so tense, I couldn't help but butt in. "What'd he say?"

"He said just because she said that didn't mean she did it."

That sure knocked all my hopes down. I was still gonna be the Sheriff's number one suspect. I looked over at Mom. Her face was stiff with trying not to show how she felt.

But Mr. Farnsworth had a little bit of good news. "Sheriff Price said that moved you down the suspect list."

I tried not to get my hopes up too far. "He got other suspects?"

"That's what he said, but of course I couldn't ask him who."

"Well, that's something, I guess." I set there pondering Junior Flint and how I was gonna get the proof.

"Let's talk about happier things," Mr. Farnsworth said. "Sheriff's team is all finished with investigating, so the crime scene tape is gone. That meant I could have the electricity turned back on, and now the gate can be opened with the remote. I had an electrician make sure everything's safe, and I'm responsible for paying the bills until the will's probated."

He laid a hand on the folder on his desk. How could a folder that slim hold so much of our future? Mr. Farnsworth went on, "Here's the promissory note. I kept it simple." He passed us each a copy. "It just says Jimmy Lee will pay me back when he gets his inheritance. Without interest." That last put smiles on me and Mom's faces. We'd forgot to think about that.

Mr. Farnsworth smiled back at us. "As I said, probate could take a year or more." He looked over at me. "You might even be eighteen then. If so, you'd be responsible as an adult to follow through. If you're still younger than that, your mother will be responsible to see I'm reimbursed out of your inheritance."

He give us a few minutes to read our copies. Took me a while to go through it, and I saw there was a blank space for the amount of the loan.

"How much will the loan be?" I asked.

"Let's figure what you would have made working for Mrs. Simmons for two years. I'll have Suzy fill in that amount," he said.

"It'll take a couple days for me to get that sum for you. Then we'll deposit it in your bank account. What bank is that?"

"Lewiston Bank," Mom said, and he said that was his bank too, so the whole thing would be simple.

So we figured out how much I woulda made, he called Miz Monroe with the amount, she put that in her computer, printed it and come in with new copies of the note. Whole thing hardly took five minutes. Meanwhile, Mr. Farnsworth offered us some coffee, but we was too nervous to have any.

Me and Mom signed all three copies of the note, Miz Monroe did her notary thing with this stamping machine, and that was it. We was gonna have enough for the family 'til the will was probated. Couldn't hardly believe our troubles was over so easy. Well, the money troubles at least. Still had the troubles of Miz Simmons being burned to death.

On the way home, me and Mom talked about what we just done. Was Miz Simmons' money gonna come through, or would something happen to keep me from getting what she left me? Once again, Mom brought her wisdom to bear. "All that's up to the Lord," she said. "We gotta trust in the Lord." And that's what we tried to do, not just that day, but every day after.

I dropped off Mom and turned round to pick up Eden after school, meaning to go to the Quik Treet so we could talk. But she told me to drive to her friend Bethanne's shop. I knew about Bethanne from Eden talking, but I never met her 'til we got to Gifts-n-Such. We went inside, and there was Bethanne and Mae, her business partner, waiting for us.

I been looking forward to meeting the woman I heard so much about, and I give Bethanne the once-over. Hard to imagine how a teenage girl and an older woman come to be friends. But solving the mystery of how their loved ones happened to die together, sharing those hardships and triumphs, all that had to bring 'em close.

Bethanne musta been over fifty and looked it. Seemed like life had treated her some kinda hard. But she also looked like she come through it, and things was looking up for her. She was wearing makeup that softened the wrinkles, and she musta just come from the beauty parlor 'cause her hair had that done-up look. Couldn't help but notice her gray slacks and sweater was just the opposite from what her business partner had on.

Mae was a large black woman, dressed in the loudest dress I ever set eyes on. Blue-and-white flowers on a maroon background. But she had more dignity than I ever saw in man or woman, and that's the truth even today. Mae went over to the door, locked it, turned over the sign to read "Closed" and motioned us all into the back room.

We set round an old wood card table. Bethanne poured us all a cup of tea and handed round the homemade biscuits. She winked at Eden. "You know I didn't make these. Mae did, but she's teaching me, slow but sure."

Mae smiled and set down in an old chair that creaked under her weight. "Homemade strawberry jam too. That's the next lesson."

I musta been looking dumbstruck, 'cause Eden said, "Jimmy Lee, two heads're better'n one. And four're better'n two. I know I said we'd talk after school, but I called Bethanne 'cause of all me and her been through." Then she stopped and corrected herself. "All she and I've been through. Figured we needed her advice too."

Bethanne laid a hand on my arm. "And I asked Mae to sit in, because she's smarter than all of us put together." Eden rolled her eyes, and Bethanne added, "Okay, nobody's smarter than Eden, but Mae's smart from life, while Eden's smart from books." Bethanne smiled. "And television, but that's another story."

Eden looked like that soothed her a bit. She asked me to tell Bethanne and Mae what I told her that morning. I was feeling off-base, setting with all them females, but I knew Eden was smart, and if she said to get on with it, get on with it I would. So I told the whole thing, starting with me going to work for Miz Simmons, through finding Lazarus and him getting killed, down to Miz Simmons being burned to death and the Sheriff suspecting me. I ended up with, "But I know Junior Flint done it, and I'm gonna get him if it's the last thing I do."

"How you know Junior did it?" Eden asked. "Even the Sheriff has other suspects. Let's not jump the gun."

I leaned back in my chair, and it creaked as much as Mae's had just a few minutes before. Them wood chairs looked as old as they sounded. Musta come outta somebody's attic. Wood all bent into curves to make the backs and legs. I crossed my arms over my chest and said, "I know Junior done it. He killed Lazarus, and he killed Miz Simmons too."

"Got some proof, do you?" Mae asked, and I had to admit I didn't, but I was gonna get it.

"How you plan to do that?" Bethanne said.

"Gonna watch him every minute of every day and night."

Eden bit her lip and looked at me like I was a five year-old. "Jimmy Lee, you can't do that. Nobody can, not 24/7. You need help, and we're gonna give it."

Bethanne reached for another biscuit and piled on the butter and jam. "I'll keep an eye on him at the Roadhouse. Just get a beer, sit in a back booth and keep my ears open. You know how folks can't keep a secret when they got too much to drink."

Eden give her a funny look and said, "I don't know that's such a good idea, Bethanne," and Mae chimed in, "Me neither."

Seemed like the two of 'em knew something I didn't, but them saying it wasn't a good idea for Bethanne to go out there wasn't gonna matter, 'cause we had Mitch. "My cousin goes out there a few times a week. Junior hasn't been coming so much, but Mitch'll let us know what he says and does."

"Okay, let's leave that to Mitch," Eden said.

"Well, all right," Bethanne said, but she didn't seem too happy about it. "I know Becky Phillips. She comes in here to buy craft materials for her hobbies. Next time she shows up, I'll steer her into talking about what she knows."

That was news to me. Didn't know Becky Phillips did anything but fool round with Junior. I was waking up to the fact that I didn't know as much as I thought I did.

And Mae's next words confirmed it. "What about Mr. Farnsworth? Did Miz Simmons ever say anything to him about why she was writing a will so early in life? Was she afraid somebody might do her harm? He's our lawyer too, but I don't see how I could bring up anything about Miz Simmons."

"No," I said, "but I can. I don't wanna bother him more'n I have to. The loan coming through will give me a reason to get back in touch. That should only take a couple days, if everything goes according to plan."

Eden leaned forward, elbows on the crowded table. "Didn't you tell me a story a while back about Hank Conner? You said there was something between him and Miz Simmons, but you didn't know what."

"That's true, but I don't know how to find out."

"I do," Mae said. "My sister keeps house for him now his wife passed. You know how we all hear things we're not supposed to, working for rich folks."

We went on like that for a while, figuring who was gonna do what. But deep in my heart, I still knew Junior done it, and I was gonna get the proof if it took the rest of my life.

12

FIRST STOP IN THE SEARCH for that proof was Orrin Dent. Decided I'd wait at the place he parked his truck before he walked on up to his pot field. So I was awake bright and early the next morning. Grabbed some bread and butter and was out the door before Mom could ask too many questions.

Pulled outta our drive and called Eden to tell her what I was gonna do.

"He's not gonna be working in his pot field this time of year," she said.

"What do you know about growing pot?" I asked. "Besides, I heard he spent the fall putting in a plastic greenhouse up there, so he can grow it year round." She was silent, so I said, "It's worth a try."

She come back like her jaw wouldn't move much. "Okay, I'll find my own way to school. But you let me know how it goes, okay?"

"Deal."

A little weak sunshine finally come out after all them days of rain, but it didn't cheer me up none. Started thinking maybe ambushing Orrin wasn't such a good idea. I remembered what happened when Miz Simmons come on him unawares, and I didn't wanna risk getting a stomach full of buckshot. But I give myself a good talking-to and went on down the road.

I parked uphill from the turnoff to the old lumber track Orrin used, let the air outta a tire and waited for him to drive by. Soon enough, I saw his ol' blue truck coming round the bend, and I waved my lug wrench for help.

Now most folks in West Virginia will come to the aid of a body in need, and Orrin was no differnt. He pulled up behind, got out and asked what he could do.

"My jack's broke, slips on the ratchet. Can I borrow yours?"

Well, he fell for it, and I felt a little shamed to be tricking him like that. Then I reminded myself it was for a good cause and went on with it.

He got his jack out and said, "You the boy was helping Miz Simmons."

I didn't like the "boy" part, but I sure was glad he brought up the subject without me having to turn the conversation from my tire to her dying. Have to admit him saying that made me feel good to be looking down on his short and stocky body from my six feet.

"That's right," I said. "Jimmy Lee Schuman."

His eyes raked me up and down, which required a little effort on his part 'cause he was so short. But he was built like a bull, and I didn't wanna give him no reason to come at me. He put a pinch of Copenhagen under his lip. "You growed up some since last time I seen you. Must be all that hard labor you been doing." He scratched at something under his shirt. "Sure was a shame to hear what happened to that widder woman. Heard you was the one found her."

I nodded. "Come up over the ridge from Lewiston and saw the cabin on fire. Wasn't nothing I could do but call 9-1-1."

He stood there talking, beating round the bush and trying to pump me for information. Made me all cautious to see how quick the tables was turned. I was careful what I said, and he finally spit out what he wanted to know. "They figure out who done it?"

I picked up my lug wrench. "Think the Sheriff's already got a list of suspects."

"Oh?" Orrin sounded as cautious as I felt. He kneeled down by my flat tire. "Who's on it?" He started jacking up the truck.

I was wondering if he had a connection with Junior I didn't know about. Other'n Junior buying pot from him. "Well, Junior Flint, for sure," I said and got down beside him, ready to do my part. "You're the one told us they was gonna put her dog's eye out."

Orrin spit a brown stream from his snuff. "Yep, but never said it was Junior."

"Well, that's who it was. We found Lazarus laying in his own blood, spiked to Junior's porch."

"Yep. Heard about that." He reached for the lug wrench, and just for a moment, I felt a little thrill of fear run up my neck. Didn't have no reason to feel like that, but somehow I did.

Help me, Lord, I prayed. Give me strength like You done before. I nodded toward the other side of the holler, the ridge that run from Junior's farm over to Miz Simmons' land. "You ever see Junior this side of the ridge?"

Orrin stopped loosening up the lugs and give me a long look. "Lotta folks go back and forth on that ridge. Hunters mostly."

I tried to smile just an ordinary smile. "Don't mean to get in your business, but you're on this ridge a lot. If someone come over the opposite side, might be you could see who it was."

"Maybe." He went back to work on the lugs.

I let him get 'em all off. Then I helped pull the flat tire away before I said anything more. "Miz Simmons told me how you two met up, had a beer and some of them delicious cookies she used to make."

Orrin give me a long look. "She was a good woman. Let me be after that." He wrestled the tire outta the way while I got my spare down. "Too bad I can't say the same for her dog."

I raised my eyebrows and waited. Orrin spit another stream of tobacco juice. "That dog was always barking, always running up to the fence. Calling attention to my business. Why couldn't she control him better?"

"She did try. That's why we built the fence."

"Didn't try hard enough." Orrin hawked his snuff into the ditch. "Let's get this job done."

I joined him down by the wheel hub. Didn't try to keep him talking 'til after the lugs was back on, and he was letting the jack down.

"So what happened?" I said. "You ever see Junior come over the ridge?"

Orrin got up, the heavy jack in his hand. "Yeah, I seen him plenty of times. Seen him squirrel hunting. Seen him prowling the fence."

I got a rag outta the back of my truck and passed it to him to wipe his hands. "What about that day? You see him the day the cabin was set on fire?"

He set the jack on the bed of his truck, wiped his hands and looked down the road toward where Miz Simmons' cabin used to be. Took his own good time doing it. Then he said, "I seen somebody come over the ridge, but they was too far away for me to know who it was." He give his head a tight little shake and me an even tighter smile. "Couldn't even swear they was coming from Junior's farm."

Orrin stood there, waiting for me to leave. I figured he didn't want me watching him drive up that old lumber track, and I was happy to oblige. But I was left to wondering what he wasn't saying. Seemed like there was stuff he was hiding. Did it have to do with Junior or with him?

So what was I gonna do next? Felt like a chicken running round in circles. It was too soon to get the loan, so I didn't have no good excuse to go talk with Mr. Farnsworth again. Had some questions for him after me and Eden talked with Bethanne and Mae, but that was gonna have to wait.

That thought made me wonder if Mae'd had time to talk with her sister. Maybe she called her last night? Maybe she still had some of them biscuits, even if they was a day old? I sure was hungry. Maybe I was still a growing boy after all.

Realized I didn't have her phone number. Or the number of the store neither. Best we all trade phone numbers next time we was together.

Drove into Lewiston and up to Gifts-n-Such round ten, just as Mae was turning the sign on the door from "Closed" to "Open." Didn't see Bethanne nowhere. Maybe she was gonna come in later.

Mae give me a big smile and waved me on in. "Glad to see you. Haven't had a chance to talk with my sister. Her baby girl's laid up with the flu, and this isn't the time to bother her with anything else."

Well, that was one more thing I couldn't do today. Mae must've seen how I was feeling, 'cause she said, "You look hungry. You hungry? Let me feed you some of the coffee cake I baked last night."

She set me down in the back room, cut me a big piece of cake, made me tea with honey, just like I was family. I coulda sworn that woman was as good a baker as Miz Stealey down at the church. And that was saying something for sure.

Wasn't long before I was outta the dumps and ready to give it another try. Thanked Mae for the cake and tea but didn't tell her where I was going. What she didn't know couldn't hurt me.

Figured it was a good time to check out what Junior was doing. Didn't want to be spotted, so I drove the long way round, past Miz Simmons' burnt-out cabin, past the dirt track where Orrin had no doubt hid his truck, round the top of the holler and over the ridge to just before Junior's farm. Parked the truck along another dirt track and climbed up the hill 'til I could see down onto his land. There wasn't much cover in them woods, just bare trunks and branches, so I couldn't get real close. But I got close enough.

Junior was loading up his truck with firewood, and that halfwit brother was getting in the way as much as he was helping. Floyd had a squeaky, high voice, and I could hear him where I was, he talked so loud. "How'm I doing, Junior? Am I doing okay? Do you want the gas can too?"

My heart started banging against my ribs. Gas? Did Sheriff Price say anything about the fire being set with gasoline? I racked my brain, but I couldn't remember.

Junior's deep voice rumbled, and Floyd said, kinda sing-songy

"Okay, Junior. Whatever you say, Junior. No gasoline this time. No gasoline. No gasoline."

They got in Junior's truck and drove off toward Lewiston. I run down to my truck, but by the time I got out on the road, I couldn't see hide nor hair of 'em. I drove into Lewiston and still didn't see 'em anywhere. Where'd they gone to? There was a couple turnoffs to other towns on that road. Maybe I missed 'em that way.

Decided I might as well make myself useful at home. Lotta things not getting done now Dad was gone. I been working to bring in cash, but now I had time to pick up all the stuff needed doing.

Mom give me peanut-butter-and-jelly sandwiches for lunch, along with apples from our trees. We always stored our apples and potatoes in barrels of straw out in the root cellar my grandaddy's grandaddy carved into the hillside out back of the house. They keep most all winter that way, only a few of 'em going bad toward summer. But by that time, the peaches is coming on, so then we'd have fresh fruit to eat.

Finished my lunch and set to work. Like a lot of folks, we got a wood stove to keep us warm in winter. That thing musta stood in our house since it was built. Does a good job too. Anyway, seeing Junior's truck put me in mind we needed more wood, so I went out back and split logs 'til the kids come home from school. All the while, my mind was singing, just like Floyd, "Gasoline. Gasoline. No gasoline this time."

13

THAT NIGHT, I CALLED EDEN and said I was looking forward to driving her to school so we could talk. Wasn't too happy about the way we parted that morning, but didn't wanna say much for fear Mom'd overhear. Didn't want her to worry about me trying to get Junior for killing Miz Simmons.

Eden seemed to hear what I was thinking by the sound of my voice. She said she had something she wanted to speak about too and rung off. No small talk like we usually done. Figured I was in the doghouse for sure and not clear what I could do to get out. I had to get Junior, but I sure was walking a fine line not telling everything to Eden and Mom. Felt like I could fall off anytime.

Then I called Mitch to set up a meet so we could talk about his watching Junior down to the Roadhouse. Once again, I couldn't say much about why I wanted to get together, but Mitch was used to Mom being the way she was and said he'd meet me after work the next day.

I got in bed under the patchwork quilt Grammy made a long time ago. In them days, people didn't make fancy quilts from new material like you see for sale along the roadside now. She cut up old clothes when they was too worn out to wear and pieced 'em together however she could make 'em fit. I look at her quilt, and I think it's our family history. A patch of a print from a dress, a patch of blue from a work shirt, even a patch from an old flour sack when they used to come sewed up in nice material.

So I laid under Grammy's quilt and thanked the Lord for a fruitful day. Lots done and still more to go. I knew He was at my side, 'cause He give me a deep and restful sleep all night long. Didn't even hear the ruckus from my sisters' room 'til Mom told me about it the next day.

That morning, I tried to get out early again, but Mom was waiting for me in the kitchen.

"Here," she said, arms crossed and face stern, "Where're you off to in such a rush? You ain't got no work now Miz Simmons is gone, and I got something needs doing here."

Lord have mercy, I thought. "Sorry, Mom. I promise to help you later this morning, but one of the tires went flat, and I wanna get it fixed before another one goes bad. I'll be back soon as I can."

She squinted and looked in my eyes. "You sure that's it?"

"Yes, ma'am." I grinned, trying to take comfort in knowing I was telling the truth. "Want me to bring you the receipt?" Just not all the truth, and that's a sin too. I needed to do me a lot of meditating on my sins. Just as soon as all this was over.

"Don't you get smart with me, young man. And bring us some salt. I'm fresh out."

I bent down to kiss her on the cheek. "Yes'm. Back before ten."

"Counting on it," she called after me as I went out the door.

When I come out, I heard Butch growling over by the rabbit hutch, so I had to go see what was the matter. Found fox prints all round the hutch but no fox. Give ol' Butch a pat on the head and told him what a good dog he was and when I got back, we'd go together to find out how that fox got in.

All that put me behind, and I had to drive to the Happy Hours Trailer Park straight away. Eden climbed in the truck without a smile or a hello. Yep, I was in the doghouse all right, but how was I gonna get out? Telling her about what I saw at Junior's the day before was definitely not gonna help. So I kept quiet and let her do the talking while I done the driving.

"Jimmy Lee, maybe you can fool Bethanne and Mae, but you can't fool me. You just went along with what everybody was saying at the shop, but you don't really want anybody's help. You're bound and determined to prove Junior did it. And all by yourself."

She was so close to the mark, I had to pull over and say my piece. "Lot of truth to that, but I hear what you-all are saying. I do think Junior done it, but I also see we need to look at every side of this." Was that gonna simmer her down? Sure hoped so.

She looked at me for a long time and said, "Well, don't jump to conclusions. If there's one thing I learned after Ray-Jean's murder, that was it. I was always leaping before I looked, and I don't wanna see you make the same mistake."

I reached out an arm across the bench seat and pulled her close as the seat belts would allow. "When're all of us gonna meet again? Should we make our meets regular or just when we have something to tell?"

She unsnapped her seatbelt and snuggled up for a minute. "Just as often as we have something to share. And that means you too. If you know something, you gotta share it."

"Deal," I said and started driving toward Lewiston High again. I sure was making a lot of promises that morning. Too many to keep?

Got back home before ten, just like I said, tire pumped up and salt bought. Spent the rest of the morning fixing the bed my sisters broke jumping up and down the night before. That was the ruckus I slept through. Mom said she never been so mad. She give 'em both a hiding and made 'em sleep on the floor. Told 'em it'd do 'em good to suffer some after what they done. Mom was strict with us, and she punished us when we done wrong, but that's one of the ways she showed her love. She was pretty free with the hugs too, when we done good.

She cooked the two of of us some fatback for lunch and warmed up some green beans she'd canned. Even fried up potatoes left over from the night before.

"What're you doing this afternoon?" she said.

"I gotta go with Butch to find out how a fox got inside the fence and all round the rabbit hutch."

Her face fell. "Them rabbits is precious. The freezer's getting low on meat. We got a lotta beans canned, but folks need meat too."

"Once we get that loan, I'll get something down at the Busy Bee." I started for the door. "Best get moving now about that fox. I gotta go see Mitch round three."

She tilted her head and give me a look. "What're you seeing him for?"

Here I go again, I thought, more half-truths. "He promised to see if there was any work for me where he is. Even with the loan, it'd be good to have more money coming in."

She grinned. "Well, let's don't drown in it." That was Mom's sense of humor, and I give it the smile it deserved.

Me and Butch found where the fox dug under the fence, and I

put in a couple of rocks and dirt. That'd have to hold 'til I could figure out something more permanent. Got cleaned up to go see Mitch and drove off with a wave from Mom. Felt like I was committing a sin an hour, even if it was for a good cause. Sure didn't wanna talk with Pastor Bob about it. Not then, anyway.

Me and Mitch got us a couple Cokes at the Quik Treet and drunk 'em in his truck so nobody'd hear what we had to say. Mitch was like a big brother to me, and I always felt like there wasn't nothing we couldn't talk about.

"You wanna know about work, Jimmy Lee?" he begun. "There's nothing to be had for miles round. I lucked out and got a roof-repair job from snow damage, but that'll be over in a few days." He shook his head. "Wish I could do more for you, but..."

"That's okay, Mitch," I interrupted 'cause I didn't want him feeling bad. "Miz Simmons left me everything, and her lawyer's gonna give us a loan to tide us over 'til the will's probated."

He looked as dumbstruck as I felt when I first got the news. "You don't mean it!" He give me a punch on the shoulder. "You son of a gun! I'm happy for you, and that's the truth. You-all had your fair share of suffering, and it sure is time for some good news."

Mitch swigged his Coke and looked like he just got an idea. "Tell you what. Maybe we ain't got no work, but that don't mean we can't eat. Let's me and you go hunting, get us some deer meat to see us through the winter."

"Mom was just telling me we need meat," I said, "but you know I ain't much of a hunter. Dad took me along once I got big enough, but I just ain't good with a gun."

Mitch patted my knee. "You ain't gonna get good if you don't work at it. What if I pick you up early Saturday morning, and we give it a try?"

"Okay. I'll dig out the camos me and Dad used." Then I changed the subject and started talking about trying to find out who killed Miz Simmons. Told him about Junior being my number one suspect. That made me realize I did see the point of Eden saying not to jump to conclusions. Sort of surprised myself when I saw if Junior was number one, then somebody else could be number two. Or three. Or four. Or...

"Anyway," I summed up, "I sure could use your help keeping an eye on him down to the Roadhouse. Maybe he'll say or do something when he's liquored up."

"You got it, J.L.," he said. "Miz Simmons was one special lady, and if Junior done it, I'll be the first one to help put him away. In fact, all this talking's made me thirsty. " He winked. "Think I'll drift out there right now."

I thought about what else I might do to move things along, but then God give me the grace to think about what I owed Mom and the kids. So I went on home, told her Mitch didn't have no work in mind for me and contented myself spending time with my brothers and sisters. They rode the school bus back and forth to Lewiston, so we only saw each other in the evenings. I was usually gone by the time they come down to breakfast. Anyway, we didn't have nearly enough time together since Dad died, so that evening was a blessing.

We didn't watch TV at our house. Had one once, but Mom and Dad decided there wasn't much worth watching, so that was the end of that. They sold it, and we none of us missed it. Sometimes, if I was over to Mitch's, we watched sports or one of them reality shows. Eden watched educational TV when she wasn't studying. But me, I read the Bible, played with the kids or talked with Mom. That pretty much made up my evenings once I wasn't so tired from working that I fell asleep after supper.

Just when I was getting ready for bed, Mitch called. He sounded a little worse for the wear, and I could hear music and shouts and cars in the background.

"Jimm' Lee," he said, "I'm out at the Roadhouse. Setting inna parking lot."

"Sounds like you had a few beers too many."

He laughed. "Tha' I did, Cuz, tha' I did. But it was for a good cause. Junior's here, even if it is Thursday. Thought for sure I wouldn't see him 'til tomorrow night. Tha's when just about everybody's here."

My heart jumped up to the rafters. "And?"

"Running his mouth about how nobody could touch him."

"Touch him for what?"

"Didn't say, but sure was proud of hisself."

There was this long pause, then a burp that must've sounded all the way to Morristown.

I was losing my patience. "What else did he say? Who was he with?"

"With that white trash Becky Phillips. Hanging all over him." Mitch let out another burp. "Scuse me." He took in a breath. "J.L.? Strangest thing. Them boils is all gone. Couldn't see a one anywhere, neck or face. Don't that beat all?"

Sounded like Mitch was taking a swig from a bottle. You could hear a gurgle, and his lips made a sucking sound when they let go.

"Mitch?" I said.

Silence. Followed by another burp, this one fit to wake the dead.

"Mitch, what else did he say?"

"Said folks better stay outta his business, or he'd get 'em for sure."

14

THE NEXT DAY WAS FRIDAY, end of the week and end of that couple days of weak sunshine. A sharp wind was blowing gray clouds across the sky like they was running away from something. But that didn't bother me none, 'cause Suzy Monroe called from Mr. Farnsworth's office to say the loan was ready and could me and Mom meet him at the Lewiston bank at eleven. That didn't give us a lotta time, but we rushed through our chores and got cleaned up to go to town.

On the way, I started to thinking about what Junior said at the Roadhouse, but I couldn't make sense of it. Something going on, but not enough for me to nail him. Maybe now his boils was gone, he'd be going down to the Roadhouse more often, and Mitch'd hear something. I just had to count on that.

Once again, Mr. Farnsworth treated us with the greatest courtesy, and I decided that no matter what I decided to do with Miz Simmons' legacy, he was gonna be my lawyer too. I been so shook up the first couple of times I been in his office, I didn't pay attention to how he looked. But now I took the time, and what I saw give me even more confidence in him. Dark hair turning gray, wire-rimmed glasses, tweed sport coat seen some wear, old shoes polished up nice. Not showing off, just being hisself. I thanked him for spending so much time with us and said I'd like to pay him for that time.

He just smiled his gentle smile, "Not necessary. I consider this part of my duty as Mrs. Simmons' attorney, fulfilling her wishes."

Well, we went into the Lewiston Bank, and we was treated like we was somebody. Not like when I went with Dad once to cash his paycheck. That teller acted like Dad was almost beneath notice. She handed over the cash and looked past him to the next customer before we even left the window. Made me feel we was small.

But this time, Mr. Farnsworth went over to the woman at the counter in front of these little cubbyholes with folks working inside. He told her who we was, and next thing I knew, we was ushered into the office of the Vice President. He stood up, give Mr. Farnsworth a big smile and a handshake, with the same for me and Mom. Sure does help to have money in this world.

Anyway, once we got down to it, the V.P. transferred the money from Mr. Farnsworth's account to Mom's. He asked if we wanted to keep any cash back, and I answered real quick, "Five hunnerd dollars."

Mom raised her eyebrows at me, so I said, "We gotta do that Christmas shopping," and she nodded. You probably noticed Mom's not much of a talker.

Everything went smooth as silk, and we walked outta the bank with more money in Mom's account than me and her ever seen, and I had five hundred dollars in my wallet. Mom said she needed to do a little shopping long as we was in town, and that give me the chance I needed to speak with Mr. Farnsworth about what we all discussed at Gifts-n-Such. I asked him if he'd like to go for a cup of coffee. Said I wanted to ask him a few questions. Seemed like the least I could do, offer him coffee, after all he done for us.

We ended up at the Corner Cafe, setting in the back booth, so I didn't have to worry none about nobody hearing. Got us each a piece of punkin pie too. First, I brought up how to manage my loan money that was in Mom's account. I was kinda uneasy I'd be like a boy again after being the breadwinner. Mr. Farnsworth suggested me and Mom could agree on how much to take out every month and divide it up according to need. That way, I wouldn't have to go to her every time I needed some cash, and Mom would have money for the mortgage and stuff I been paying for when I worked.

That took a load off my mind, so I went on to the questions Mae brought up when we all had our meeting. "Miz Simmons wasn't that old. She ever say anything about why she wanted to write a will so early in life?"

Mr. Farnsworth shrugged. "I encourage all my clients to write wills. Even the young ones. Especially if they have a family. You never know what life will bring. Once you're grown up, you're old enough to write a will."

That got me to thinking. Maybe I should write a will. What if Junior come for me too? How'd I know Mom and the kids'd get what Miz Simmons left me? Decided to think on that some more and come back to Mr. Farnsworth when I was ready.

For now, best keep focused on why Miz Simmons had a will. "She ever say she was afraid somebody might do her harm? Especially after they killed her dog?"

He shrugged again. "Not to me. Writing that will was just normal, as far as I could see. She didn't have any living relatives. I brought up gifts to charities, but she said she'd rather give everything to you."

Just then, Mom come into the Corner Cafe to meet up like we agreed. She said she needed to be getting on home, so we said our goodbyes to Mr. Farnsworth and headed for the truck. On the way back to our house, I told her his idea about how to manage the loan money.

"I been thinking the same thing," she said. "That's your money in the bank, and we should use it like you want."

"Well, that's what I want," I said. "Every month, you get what I already been bringing in to pay for whatever, and I get cash for what I need." I pulled up in front of the house. "Here's an example. The seat cover on this old truck is falling apart. What if I go over to Gmart and use some of that five hunnerd dollars to buy a new one?"

She give me a pat on the arm, picked up her shopping and said, "So what're you waiting for?"

I give her a smile and a wave and headed for the Gmart parking lot. Before I got outta the truck, I sent Eden a text suggesting we all meet the next day, if that'd work out for everybody. Then I went inside and put the prettiest comforter I could find, all roses and ivy, on layaway, so Mom'd have the best Christmas I could give her. I bought that seat cover for Dad's truck and fastened it on right then and there in the parking lot. Didn't get the most expensive one, but it looked good, and what's more, it'd wear good.

While I was covering up all the grease and grime and holes in the seat, I got to thinking about Eden and how I never had the money to give her nothing. So I went back inside and over to the jewelry counter. I was looking for something could be a sign of how I felt about her, but everything was too expensive. Finally, way at the back of the case, I saw a tiny little silver heart on a thin, silver chain-bracelet. Wished it could be more. Bigger and made of gold, but I settled for what I could afford. Told myself Mom always said it's the thought that counts.

Drove on home, showed Mom the new seat cover and called the

repairman to come fix the fridge. That sure brought a smile to her face, and we set up a date for us to go Christmas shopping for my brothers and sisters. Then I patched up some doors and cupboards that needed fixing and played with the kids when they come home from school. Eden called after supper to say we could all meet at the shop once it closed at five. So that was another good day the Lord give me.

But the good luck ended early Saturday morning. I was up and dressed in my camos, Dad's rifle and ammo at the ready, when Mitch called to say we wasn't going hunting after all. He just got home from the Emergency Room. He worked a one-day construction job on Friday and took a fall from a ladder at the end of the day. Made me wonder if he been too hung over from the night before. Nothing broke, but he hurt his back real bad. Doc put him in a brace and told him to stay home 'til it was better. Wasn't just hunting that wasn't gonna happen. There went Friday nights at the Roadhouse. Mitch never made it out there that night, and he wasn't going anytime soon.

Wasn't nothing to do but go on to the meet that afternoon and hope we could solve that problem. Truth to tell, I was also hoping for some more good baking, and I sure wasn't disappointed. Mae had blueberry muffins for everybody along with fresh coffee. Couldn't help but wonder if Mae'd teach Eden how to make some of them things once they both had time.

First thing we done was trade phone numbers so we could keep in touch whenever we needed to. Then I told what Mr. Farnsworth said about it being normal for Miz Simmons to write a will, and there wasn't no hint of her being scared somebody was gonna do her harm.

Eden had a notebook, and she was writing down everything we said.

Mae give a report on her talk with her sister about Hank Conner, and there sure was a story to tell. Turned out Conner held a grudge against Miz Simmons. He was her dad's partner in real estate and banking. But her dad died young, and Conner cheated his family outta their inheritance. Said he'd invest their money and help 'em double it in a year. Then he told 'em the real estate deal went bust, and they was left having to live with a lot less'n they planned on. Conner thought he'd really pulled off a fast one 'til Miz Simmons wrote about it in one of her books. She changed the names and some of the details, but everybody in Lewiston read that book and knew what Hank Conner done to her family. Mae's sister heard Conner shouting about it when he come home not long after the book come out. Said he was mad enough to kill.

Bethanne spoke up. "Why didn't Conner sue Miz Simmons?"

"Dunno," Mae said, "Maybe he thought taking her to court would just prolong the gossip. Probably hated to lose out on getting revenge money out of her, but the gossip hurt more."

"When did that book come out?" Eden asked.

"Five years, maybe more," Mae answered, and Eden scribbled it down.

Bethanne shook her head. "That was a long time ago. Why'd he want to kill her now, after all this time'd passed?"

Eden stopped writing and looked up. "Maybe we don't know enough yet. Let's keep our suspicions about Hank Conner open."

Bethanne grinned. "I talked to Becky Phillips. That woman sure is slippery. I kept trying to get her to gossip about Junior, but she kept changing the subject. I think she knows something, but she doesn't want to say." Bethanne winked. "But I'm not done yet. I'll keep after her."

"I got some news about Junior," I said. Then I told 'em what Mitch heard down to the Roadhouse and ended with him being laid up for a while.

"No problem," Bethanne said. "I'll go and see what I can find out. Becky did say they go out there every Friday."

I caught Mae and Eden giving each other a look. "Not real happy about you going out there," Eden said. "Me neither," Mae chimed in.

Bethanne looked from one to the other. "I know what you're thinking, but I'm reformed. I'll just nurse a beer and see what I can see."

I looked a question at Eden, but she just shook her head like we was going to talk about that later. We was supposed to be meeting to share information, but there sure was turning out to be a lot of stuff we wasn't gonna talk about.

Decided maybe I could bring it up after church on Sunday. The skies was still gray when I drove the whole family over, but at least I didn't have to fight the wind no more. Eden was there for Bible Study and Services. Pastor Bob preached a real good sermon on the sins of omission, so on target I was feeling guilty about all the things I hadn't done, not telling the full truth to Mom or to Eden neither.

Afterwards, me and Eden went together to the Social. Took our cake and hot tea over to a corner so we could talk off to ourselves. I had that little heart bracelet wrapped up in tissue paper in my pocket. Looked round to make sure nobody was watching and pulled it out.

"I wish I could give you something all gold and diamonds, but this little heart says it all," I said.

By the time I finished, she had it unwrapped. Her eyes got all big, and her lip kinda trembled. "Jimmy Lee, I don't know what to say."

"Don't say nothing," I said and put it round her wrist. "Just wear it."

We both musta felt like folks was looking at us, 'cause Eden changed the subject. "I know you're wondering what Mae and I are worried about when it comes to Bethanne going out to the Roadhouse."

I nodded, not wanting to break in.

"But it's not my place to tell," she said, and my hopes sunk. She put a hand on my arm and looked me in the face. "How about if I tell you if and when it's necessary?"

"Okay," I said. "I understand. I can live with that." And I meant it, but I also have to say I felt like I was getting let off the hook. If Eden wasn't gonna tell me everything unless it was necessary, then I didn't have to talk about Junior and Floyd neither. I didn't want to worry her more'n I had to about what I was doing.

15

SPENT A LOTTA THE NEXT week doing chores round the house and farm. Trying to catch up on all the things left undone since Dad died and while I was working full time. Weather turned bad with more cold rain, but I kept at it and ended up with a lot to show for my efforts.

Did my best to stay outta Sheriff Price's way, and he didn't seem to wanna have nothing to do with me neither. At least for now. But I was left to wondering what he was doing. Looking into other suspects? Trying to get the goods on me? Following up leads? What leads? No way I was gonna tell him what we was finding out, not 'til we had Junior sewn up tight and ready for delivery to the regional jail.

If I didn't kill him myself. But that woulda been stupid. Had to keep reminding myself of that. Stupid to kill Junior and ruin my life. And Mom's. And the kids'. And Eden's. I tried to bury that kinda revenge way down deep, so it couldn't rear its head in the night to destroy me and all the folks I loved.

Nobody else on the team seemed to have anything to report, 'cause none of 'em called for a meet. That meant no chance to try more of Mae's baked goods, and I sure was feeling sorry for myself.

Mom's all right as far as basic cooking goes, but she ain't no baker. Don't mean to complain or criticize, just stating a fact.

I paid Mitch a visit Tuesday afternoon. He was in a lotta pain, even with that Percocet they give him. Asked what I could do for him, and he said, "Get me more of these here pills." That give me a turn, 'cause I know how bad them pills can be once you try to go of 'em.

Didn't wanna answer, so I changed the subject. "Sorry we couldn't go hunting. I was looking forward to spending some time together, even if I can't hit the side of a barn with a gun."

"Once I get up and running, we'll try again." He grinned. "We need to get you some practice so you can at least hit the barn door." I laughed and started to say my goodbyes. Mitch added, "Sister's husband got a couple bucks last week. Said he wanted to give me one. We'll split it, you and me. That way, we'll both have us some deer meat." I begun to say that wasn't right, but he cut me off, said we was kin, and he'd let me know when it was ready.

After being with Mitch, I followed Hank Conner home from the bank, just to see where he lived and how he behaved. He had the only metallic green Cadillac Escalade in the county, so it was easy. Course my truck stuck out some in Conner's fancy neighborhood, but I hoped he'd think it was just some workman driving to a late repair job. Conner just acted normal, like a man going home after work. Smoked his pipe and went on down the streets 'til he got there and let hisself into his big ol' brick mansion. He never loosened his tie or took off his ritzy felt hat with a brim. Looked like he was too upright to let go and relax as long as anybody might see him.

Me and Mom went out to Gmart on Wednesday and bought some real nice things for the kids' Christmas, just like we planned. Course

I never said a thing about the comforter, and I managed to keep her away from the bedding department in case the clerk'd recognize me and say something. You can't put much over on Mom, but it felt like I managed to that time.

Anyway, I steered her over to the groceries section, and we got us a turkey and all the trimmings for Thanksgiving. Well, not all the trimmings. We already had stuff from our garden Mom put up in summer, tomatoes and peaches and green beans. And potatoes in the root cellar. But we bought stuffing mix and a couple punkin pies plus some lettuce. Have to say that store-bought lettuce in winter don't begin to compare with what we get outta our garden in summer. Still, you gotta eat greens year round, so it had to do. We ended up having as good a Thanksgiving as we could without Dad there to say grace.

I had money left over after all that Gmart shopping, so on Friday, I snuck out to Gmart and put a little more on what I owed for Mom's comforter. I didn't wanna make Mom suspicious by paying it all off at once and then needing more cash. Besides, we always bought big things on layaway, and somehow doing that for Mom's comforter made it seem like I was coming closer and closer, little by little, to making her life a little better.

So the week passed without nothing happening on the investigating front. But come Friday, Eden called after midnight. She was sobbing. "Jimmy Lee, I need you to come to the hospital right now. Bethanne's in an awful way, and we don't know what's gonna happen."

Got there as fast as I could and bust through the Emergency Room doors. That ol' hospital smell hit me, full of harsh chemicals and God-knows-what. Had to swallow hard just to get past it. Eden was setting in the waiting room with her momma, and my girl jumped up, run over and grabbed me round the waist. I just held her for a while, 'cause she didn't seem able to get any words out.

Mae was there with her husband. He held out a hand that was missing three fingers. I remembered Eden saying something about Mae's husband being in some accident. I kept one arm round Eden and shook his hand, all the while trying not to let on I noticed them missing fingers.

"My name's James," he said, "just like yours, but folks call me Jim."

Mae smiled, "Big Jim on account of him being so tall." And he was, maybe six-foot-six and two hunnerd twenty pounds, all muscle. Mae looked positively dainty beside him.

"What happened?" I asked her.

Mae got on the other side of Eden, put an arm through hers and led us both back to Eden's momma in the setting area. Miz Jones looked up with tears in her eyes and said, "Bethanne's been beat up so bad they don't know if she's gonna make it."

My whole body felt like somebody hit me with a cattle prod. "Who done it? Was she down to the Roadhouse?" They nodded. "Did Junior do this?"

Eden finally found her voice. "Not Junior. Somebody else. Near as anybody can tell, some guy picked her up." She paused, like she didn't wanna go on, and I set her down on the slick couch next to her momma.

Miz Jones finished, "They went to a motel and..." she glanced at Eden. "... and had sex. During or after, nobody knows, he beat the hell outta her. Left her for dead and lit out."

Just then the double doors on the far side of the waiting room opened, and a doctor come out, dressed all in green with a green cap and a white mask hanging round his neck. He give us this bitty little smile, barely moved his face. "Who's next of kin?"

Seemed like all of us was holding our breath. "Nobody," Mae finally answered. "All her kin are dead or moved away. We're the only family she's got."

The doctor looked at us, rag-taggle bunch such as we was, and give his head the tiniest shake. "Okay. She's alive." Everybody let out some kinda sound of relief and hope. He held up a hand. "But she's under sedation and in Intensive Care."

"Can we go see her?" Eden blurted out.

He smiled his bitty smile again, just the barest twitch. "Normally only family can visit, but I'm going to make an exception. You-all decide who's going to represent this...family, and I'll let that person—and only that person—in for a few minutes. After that, we'll see how things go." He turned toward the doors. "I'll send a nurse out in a few minutes. She'll take whoever you choose to ICU."

His back wasn't even through the doors before Eden said, "I'm going in. Bethanne is my best friend, and I gotta be there for her."

Both Mae and Eden's momma shook their heads, but it was Miz Jones who spoke up. "No, you're not going, Eden. I expect you know all kinds of things that girls didn't know when I was your age. What's happened to Bethanne is about the worst thing that can happen to a woman, and you've already heard a lot about it."

Eden was looking more and more stubborn as her momma went on, but Miz Jones wasn't done yet. "I'm the alcoholic in this bunch." She looked round the group. "Ain't none of you know what Bethanne's gone through." She stood up. "But I do, and I'm the one to go."

The nurse come through the doors, and Miz Jones looked down

at Eden. Her voice got all gentle. "You know I'm right, Eden. Deep down in your heart, you know I'm right."

Eden started to speak, but her momma patted her on the shoulder, nodded at the nurse and followed her down the hall.

I set down next to Eden, seat still warm where Miz Jones been sitting. Took Eden's hand and said, "I think I know what you didn't wanna tell me. Bethanne is a alcoholic, so you and Mae didn't want her to go down to the Roadhouse."

Mae crossed her arms and leaned forward. "And now look what's come of it. We never should've let her go."

Big Jim was setting next her and put a hand on her crossed arms. "Mae, Bethanne is a grown woman. Couldn't nobody stop her if she was of a mind to."

Eden was setting there, kinda white-faced, her head down. She let go of my hand and started playing with the bracelet I give her, turning it round and round on her arm. "Everybody's right. And everybody's wrong. Bethanne never shoulda gone. She can't stop drinking once she starts, even if she thinks she can. But what was... were...we gonna do to stop her? Tie her down?" Tears started running down Eden's cheeks, and she wiped 'em away with the back of her hand. "And Momma's right. She's the one to go see Bethanne, 'cause she's lived through pretty much the same thing. Maybe Bethanne's not awake, but she'll feel a kindred spirit near and know you can get through this and come out the other side."

Course Miz Jones come back in short order from visiting Bethanne. All she could say was Bethanne was deep asleep from the medicine they give her and there wasn't nothing we could do except pray. And we done a lot of that, first holding hands and saying the Lord's Prayer together, then each of us praying our own silent thoughts to the Lord.

We moved to the ICU waiting room and set up the rest of the night, taking turns getting coffee and drinks from the vending machine. Trying to give each other hope. I hardly left Eden's side all them hours, just wanted to comfort her, if I couldn't do nothing else.

When six o'clock come and day just started to show faint gray light, I went outside and called Mom, so she wouldn't worry when she found me gone. Told her what happened, and she said not to worry, I was where the Lord wanted me to be. And she'd pray too.

Miz Jones called her nephew Buck round the same time to check on how her son Cruz was doing. She left him with Buck and his girlfriend when the call come about Bethanne being in the hospital. Turned out Bethanne's purse had a list of who to call in case of emergency. Eden and Mae were on it, so that explained how come the cops got in touch.

Anyway, Buck said not to worry, Cruz could stay as long as he needed to. He and Vicki was praying too, so that was a lot of folks asking the Lord's help for Bethanne all through the night and day.

The public cafeteria opened at seven, and we all trooped in for a bite to eat, even though we wasn't feeling too hungry. Food tasted like sawdust to me, and I expect to everybody else too. But it sure beat them vending machines, and we knew we had to keep our strength up.

We was heading back to the ICU waiting area when Sheriff Price showed. He give me the once-over. I didn't know how to take that look, but I knew I was where I had a right to be and stood my ground. But keeping respectful to the law. Always pays, Dad used to say, and I figured that was never more true than now.

Miz Jones said, "I been in to see her, and she ain't awake yet. Won't be awake for some time, maybe not even today." She looked at the Sheriff like she had every right to ask, "So what'd you find out?"

Sheriff Price give us all that tough cop look and said, "None of you is kin. I'm here to see the doctor."

"Bullshit," Miz Jones said, and Eden looked at her with eyes and mouth wide open. "We already been through this with the doctor. Her sister's dead. Her nephew and niece moved away with their families not long after that. Couldn't take the gossip ruining their kids' lives." She took a step forward. "You know that as well as I do, Jerry Price."

She softened her voice. "We're as much kin as Bethanne's got. And we got a right to know what you found out."

The Sheriff rocked back on his heels, took his hat off and scratched his head, put his hand inside his collar and rubbed the back of his neck. Finally he found what he needed to say. "Okay, it'll come out later today anyway. We're interviewing everyone we can find who was at the Roadhouse. So far, nobody knew the guy. Stranger in town. He signed the register 'Bill Smith' and gave a false license number. We checked it, and no such number exists. He's long-gone, and we'll probably never catch him."

Big Jim shifted his weight, and Mae put a hand on his arm. "Thank you, Sheriff," she said. "It helps to know, even if it's bad news."

Eden spoke up. "What about the room? Dust for prints? Find anything he might've left behind?"

"Every surface wiped clean and nothing left, not even a candy wrapper," he said. "Life isn't like those shows you see on the TV. Bad guys watch those shows too. They know what we're looking for."

He hitched up his pants. "Now if you folks'll excuse me, I gotta go see the doc."

The morning wore on. Mae and Big Jim left to open the shop. Miz Jones had to go work her shift. That left me and Eden to set there through the day, having lunch in the cafeteria, peeping through the glass door of ICU, praying a lot.

Evening come, and they switched on the lights. Mae and Big Jim and Miz Jones come back, and we all had supper in the cafeteria. I called Mom again, and she told me to stay as long as I felt I was needed.

It started to snow outside, soft flakes drifting down. I looked out the window, and they seemed like tiny angels come to bring us a blessing. I spoke to the Lord in my heart, told Him how much we needed that blessing, needed our friend to come back to us, whole and well. And still the snow come down, harder and harder, 'til all the world was turned white and gleaming in the street lamps.

We was asleep when the nurse come outta ICU. We was that tired even though it wasn't yet ten o'clock. Bethanne had woke up and asked to see Eden. I got up to go too. Didn't want Eden to have to face that by herself, but the nurse give me a firm shake of the head, and Big Jim put a hand on my shoulder.

It was probably only minutes, but it seemed like hours before Eden come out.

"How is she?" "What'd she say?" "She gonna be all right?" The questions seemed to batter Eden so she couldn't stand up.

Eden sunk down onto the couch beside me and said. "Bethanne's kinda out of it. They got her on some serious pain killers. Nurse says she's gonna make it, though. Her face is all bandaged up, and her eyes are black and blue. One of 'em is swollen shut. But she grabbed my hand and held on like she was gonna drown."

"Did she say anything?" Mae asked. "What'd she say?"

Eden looked at me. "Said Junior was crowing his boils're gone now the witch's dead."

16

I THOUGHT ABOUT HOW BETHANNE paid a heavy price to find that out. Didn't seem worth it, risking her life over them words. But now we had 'em, we was bound to honor her sacrifice and use 'em. "That's another strike against Junior," I said. "He's practically bragging he killed Miz Simmons."

"Or just bragging," Big Jim said. "Running his mouth to sound tough."

"Either way," Eden said, "We still don't really know anything. Besides, we got to concentrate on Bethanne now. Get her well, then get whoever killed Miz Simmons."

I couldn't agree with that. No reason I could see not to keep on trying to prove Junior done it while we waited for Bethanne to heal. But there wasn't no need to bring all that up when Eden's feelings was so high.

So I said, "Now she's doing better, we don't all of us need to be here. Let's work out a schedule, so there's always somebody with her. Except at night, when we all need to sleep."

"I don't want her to be alone at night neither," Eden said and then give her head a couple tiny shakes. Her voice sounded like she was put out with herself. "Either."

Her momma come back with the truth. Eden couldn't skip school for days on end. And even if her brother Cruz was in nursery school down at the church, he'd need watching now and then when Miz Jones had to work.

Eden always been a pretty practical girl, and she seemed to see the wisdom of that. She got out a little notebook from her purse, and we all signed up to set outside ICU waiting for news of Bethanne, as our duties would allow. Then we went home to our beds, driving extra careful through that white world the angels made for us.

Turned out Bethanne was moved outta ICU the next day, so that meant we could take turns setting with her in a regular room. I'd already signed up to come by after church. Eden didn't show up for Services, nor her momma neither. I figured they both went to the hospital even though it wasn't their turn. Or maybe they just needed to sleep in.

Whatever, I sure missed seeing Eden. Pastor Bob seemed to pick up on my feelings, 'cause he asked if something was troubling me when we shook hands by the church door. Told him a good friend was in the hospital, and I needed to get on over there. But down in my heart, I knew I was telling him just part of the story, 'cause I couldn't face up to talking with him about all my sins just yet.

When I got to Bethanne's room, Mae was setting there, holding Bethanne's good hand while she slept. Mae was still dressed in her Sunday finest, pink wool suit and great big hat with pink feathers. She put a finger to her lips, motioning me to keep quiet.

I tiptoed past the first bed where some woman was sleeping and over to Bethanne's bed by the window. Made me feel good to know she could look out and see that beautiful winter world. Had to be a good thing, even if one eye was swelled shut.

Mae pointed to the cast on Bethanne's arm from shoulder to fingers and whispered, "Broke that in three places. She must've been trying to defend herself, holding it up to protect her head. Or maybe her body. They had to take her spleen out, because it was ruptured. Her stomach's black and blue where he kicked her. Man must be a maniac."

Just then Big Jim come through the door. Mae hugged me goodbye, and I set in the chair where she kept watch. Some of the bandages was off Bethanne's face, but it was still black and blue with nasty scratches starting to heal here and there.

First thing I done was pick up Bethanne's hand and say a little prayer. Said it out loud, in case she could hear me even while she slept.

Then I leaned back and thought about what I needed to do to bring Junior to task. How was I gonna get more'n Floyd talking about gasoline and Junior bragging down to the Roadhouse? "Talking's not doing," that's what the Sheriff kept saying. I was gonna have to go out and get some real proof. Had to keep on watching Junior, hoping he'd make a mistake. Especially now we didn't have no one to go to the Roadhouse what with both Mitch and Bethanne laid up. I had to go back out to Miz Simmons' too, see what I could see. Sure, the Sheriff and his men and the firemen been all over that place, but they didn't know it like I did. They might not find what I could.

The idea of going out to that burned cabin filled me with the heebie-jeebies. Yeah, I been to get Miz Simmons' ashes and spread 'em alongside of Lazarus's. That left me tormented for days, but I knew I had to get used to the idea of going out there, because someday it'd all be mine.

That set me to thinking about what I was gonna do with all Miz Simmons left me. The land, the bank account and the money still coming in from book sales, all that had to be a lot. It come to me I could go back to school, maybe even college. I could make my dream of becoming a preacher come true. But I never was one for book-learning. That was more for Eden, not me. I'm a doer, not a reader. Well, I didn't have to decide right then, but I sure had me a lot to think about.

Bethanne stirred in her sleep, and I took her hand again, so she'd know she wasn't alone. My touch seemed to wake her. She licked her lips and looked round. "Water," she said, and I brought the big plastic glass with a bent straw to her swollen lips. She looked at me for a while like she didn't know who I was. "Jimmy," she finally whispered, "Jimmy Lee. Eden's friend." Then she drifted back off, leaving me to breathe in that ol' hospital disinfectant smell. And pondering my crusade to get Junior if it was the last thing I done.

She about half woke up one more time while I was there and muttered one word. "Careful." I didn't rightly know what to make of that. Was she talking to me or to herself? Meanwhile, this weird voice on the intercom was saying, "Code blue, code blue."

Monday come, and Eden went back to school, just like her momma wanted. I drove her to class on roads cleaned up by the snowplows. Then I decided to go on out to Miz Simmons' cabin like I been thinking. Passed Junior's house, slowed to a crawl and give it a good look but didn't see no one to home. The roads wasn't as clean out in the country, and they was a little slick where the snow been tamped down into ice.

Started over the ridge and into the holler, when Hank Conner's metallic green Caddy come roaring up the road and over the line. It only missed hitting me 'cause I swung hard onto the berm, all the while praying I wasn't gonna go over the hillside. Conner never looked back, just kept on going like I was invisible. Had to ask the Lord to keep me from saying what I was thinking. No point casting aspersions on the man's mother.

Well, if I didn't have the willies before, I sure did after that. Felt like I coulda been killed, sliding on that slick road over into the holler. Then what woulda become of Mom and the kids? Sure slowed down the rest of the way to Miz Simmons' cabin and took my time getting through the gate and parking the truck. Set there awhile, breathing in and out real slow like Dad taught me to calm my mind. And thanking the Lord I was still alive.

I finally felt peace come over me, and I could focus on why I come. I set out to search every inch of that place, house and grounds, certain the deputies and firemen had to overlooked something. The fire'd touched some of the trees near the cabin, so the snow come through and covered the ground. But a lotta the trees down in the holler was big old pines, and the snow wasn't so thick away from that destruction.

Couldn't face the house yet, so I went round back and stood over where I'd scattered the ashes of my dear friends. Couldn't really see them ashes, 'cause they been covered by the snow, but I knew they was there. Promised Lazarus and Miz Simmons once again I was gonna get 'em justice.

Then I walked up to the head of the holler and criss-crossed back and forth, covering just about every speck of her land except the bank opposite the road. That bank was almost like a wall, it was so steep. Didn't seem like nobody was gonna climb up there.

Passed the place where the fox dug up bones and where we found Lazarus near to dying with a wire round his neck. Passed where we planted daffodils and where we fixed the fence after Junior and whoever come with him cut it. Passed here and there and found exactly nothing. No gasoline can, no box of matches, nothing.

Told myself I wasn't done yet and went over to where the back door of the cabin woulda been and up the steps. I looked across to where the front door used to be and saw footprints. Somebody come with a broom and swept the snow off the ashes, and there was footprints all over the place, crossing back and forth inside just like I crossed back and forth outside. For sure, them footprints wasn't there the day I gathered Miz Simmon's ashes. Even worse, the ashes was pushed here and there by that broom, like maybe there been something under 'em.

Somebody been looking for something. But who? Hank Conner? What would he be looking for? Wasn't nothing left of that cabin but bits of walls and lots of ashes. Even most of them thick old floorboards was gone. Did he think Miz Simmons had a strongbox under her cabin? Hid in some hole? Sure didn't seem like something a bank president would do.

But you come out to look for something, I told myself. Looking for something left behind. Was that it? Did Junior leave something he had to get before anybody else found it? Did he find it or not? I did my best to go through all them ashes, front to back and side to side, but I never found nothing. Just like outside, nothing to be found.

I got a piece of tarp outta the truck and put it on one of the overturned logs so I could set there and stay dry. Dug a toe under the leaves, some covered with snow, all of 'em piled deep. They was wet and moldy underneath, and the ground itself was wet and muddy. A smell rose up, that thick winter-rot smell that promises rich earth in the spring. Overhead, some chickadee was calling out his two notes, happy to be alive on a winter morning.

But I sure didn't feel that way. I bent over, elbows on knees, head in hands, eyes closed, feeling like I was an idiot to think there was anything to find. My eyes was burning, and I was afraid I was gonna start blubbering. So I rubbed 'em good and looked out across to the creek to the steep bank that run up the ridge and on over to Junior's farm.

It come to me I been taking too much for granted about nobody being up there. Shook my head and got a move on. Figured it'd be easier to search coming down than going up, so I climbed from the gate along the fence and then did the same old criss-cross, holding onto vines and saplings to keep my balance. I did find a tiny bit of a trail, but it coulda been anything, fox maybe, it was that narrow.

Followed the trail to a hole under a rock shelf. That just about confirmed my suspicion, fox or some such. Then I saw it, spilled on the rock. Tobacco, just a few bits so wet and and torn by wind you couldn't even tell what kinda tobacco it been. Not a cigarette, that was for sure. But it coulda been from a pouch or a tin. And Junior loved his chaw.

I was leaning over to gather it up, give it a sniff and try to learn more when two things happened at the same time. I heard the shot and saw the tobacco fly in all directions. Then come another shot. Whizzed by my ear so close I felt the breeze of it. I knew who had that rifle. He was over on the other side of the holler, and I wasn't about to give him another chance. I jumped far as I could, down the hillside and behind a big ol' tree. Another shot come, this time into the tree, and I felt like I was pinned down. Junior was gonna kill me for sure, just like he killed Lazarus and Miz Simmons.

17

I WAS BREATHING SO HEAVY, what with the fear and the jump, I couldn't hardly hear nothing. Leaned against that big ol' tree like a baby leaning against his momma, trying to decide whether it was safer to stay put or get outta there. Tried to still my breath and listen.

The chickadee'd stopped singing, and the only thing I heard was water dripping from snow melting up in the trees. No shot. No twigs snapping while he moved round to get a better chance. That really give me the heebie-jeebies. What was he doing? Junior was famous as a hunter, always bringing home whatever he had in his rifle sight. Was he stalking me now? Was I gonna be brought down like some deer?

My heart was beating so hard, it felt like my chest was gonna bust open. Knew I had to do something or die right there. So I dropped down and crawled for my life. Slithered on my belly like a snake through them cold, wet leaves. Praying to God to let me live, trying to keep rocks and trees and humps between me and the other side of the holler, no matter where Junior might be.

My nose was practically buried in them rotted leaves, and cold mud seeped through my jacket and jeans. Never felt so miserable in all my life. But I crawled on and on, all the while waiting for that fatal shot to ring across the holler.

Took maybe half an hour to get back to the truck, but it felt like half a day. Got inside and thanked the Lord not another round was fired. Did Junior give up? Did he just not get a good shot 'cause I was on my stomach, crawling through the mud and snowmelt? Whatever it was, I breathed a prayer of thanks, turned the key in the ignition, opened the gate with the remote and shot outta there like a bat outta hell. And that's what it been for me, hell on earth, crawling through the mud and waiting for Junior to shoot me dead.

Drove on down the mountain, away from the holler, away from where he might still be waiting for me. But if he was figuring to get me when I come by on the way to Lewiston, I fooled him good. Drove the long way home, through Moorestown and Bealton, circled round the county 'til I come to PayLo and could clean up some in the men's room.

But my clothes was a mess, even cleaning up the best I could. Knew I couldn't let Mom see me like that, so I drove on to Gmart and got some new jeans and a quilted winter jacket. Tried to tell myself that old jacket was wore out, so I wouldn't feel so bad about ruining it. Dad got it at the Army-Navy Store years ago and give it to me when he gained some weight. I been wearing it a lot since he passed, even if it was close to being a rag. Even so, I felt guilty them seams was tore apart for good.

Mom was fixing lunch when I got home. All the kids was at school except for the baby. I dropped my sack of dirty clothes, and the smell of rotted leaves filled the room. She took one look at me, turned off the fire under the pans and held out her arms. That did it. Sixteen years old and for sure a baby leaning against my momma.

She didn't say a word, just held me 'til I could talk. Then we set down at the table, and I told her the whole story. Her mouth bit in a straight line, getting harder the more I told. I figured she was gonna tell me to back off, but all she said was, "Jimmy Lee, you need you a hot meal." Then she put the pans back on the fire, heated up last night's supper, and we set down to the comfort of food and family.

When we finished eating, Mom said, "You're a grown man now. I'm not gonna tell you what to do. You gotta figure this out for yourself." Then she got up to wash the dishes, and I went outside and chopped wood 'til I couldn't chop no more.

When Lewiston High let out, I was there to pick up Eden. Told her I needed to talk to her about something important. She said she had some time before she had to be home, so I drove us over to the Quik Treet. We got us a couple hot chocolates and set in the truck.

I told her everything, starting with being run off the road, then my search, finding the ashes all messed up and ending with Junior trying to kill me.

"Jimmy Lee, you don't know it was Junior. Coulda been anybody."

That got my goat, and she musta seen it, 'cause she reached out and give me a big hug. Held on a long time, and I did my best to keep my anger in and remember she was trying to help.

Once I felt I could talk without shouting, I said, "Had to be Junior. Who else would leave a chaw on the hillside? Who else would be up there with a rifle? "

She stroked my hand and said, "Junior's not the only man who uses tobacco in this county. You gotta give up your fixation on him. Orrin rubs snuff. Hank Conner smokes a pipe. You said you couldn't tell what kind of tobacco it was."

"Who else is a good enough shot to hit that tobacco? Trying to destroy the evidence."

She smiled and kept her voice soft. "You don't know that either. Might've been a lucky shot. Probably aiming for you and missed."

I was feeling more stubborn than any mule ever thought about being. Crossed my arms and said, "Junior's the best shot in the county."

"We know Orrin has a rifle. You saw it a while back. Bet Hank Conner does too. Hardly a man here doesn't go hunting. Conner almost ran you off the road. Maybe he come...came...back to finish you off."

Her correcting herself caught my attention. She been doing that a lot lately, trying to change how she talked. Kinda got me even more upset. Who was she trying to be?

Eden went on, "What was Hank Conner doing up there anyway? Was he the one looking for something in the ashes?"

Well, we carried on like that for a while, me insisting it had to be Junior, and her just as strong it could be somebody else. I sure had to do some praying not to let her see how mad her acting that way made me. Whose side was she on anyhow?

Dropped her off at the trailer and give her a hug, but it felt stiff to me. Expect it felt that way to her too, 'cause she said, "You know you oughta tell Sheriff Price about this, Jimmy Lee. He needs to know the facts too."

That tore up trying to hug and feel better. "Bye," I said and drove off.

The further I drove, the more I realized I was mad at her and mad at myself. Just mad all round. Then another thought come to me. If I was getting shot at, I needed to make sure Mom and the kids was gonna be taken care of. I needed Mr. Farnsworth to write me a will right away.

Too late in the day to go see the lawyer, but next morning I went by his office and told him I what I wanted. Once again, he give me his warm smile and a handshake. And once again, he had to explain to me that I was basically too young to do anything legal. That left me feeling pretty bad, but his next words pepped me up. Turned out Mom would get what Miz Simmons left me even if I died before her will was probated. That's the law. Once I turned eighteen, I could write a will, name anybody I wanted to, and it'd be legal in any court of law.

But Mr. Farnsworth wasn't done. "Jimmy Lee, would you like to sign something so your mother would know you were thinking of her? Just like we did with the loan note? Your signatures aren't legally binding now, but you might feel better knowing you had your wishes down on paper."

I couldn't help but break out in a grin. "Yessir, that's exactly what I'd like to do. Thank you for being so thoughtful of my feelings."

So he said he'd write up something, and Miz Monroe would call me when it was ready. That just cinched it. Mr. Farnsworth was gonna be my lawyer no matter what.

Making sure the family'd be okay got me to thinking about Mitch. Hadn't been by to see him in a while, so why not now? Pulled up in front of his little house, four rooms and a porch. Tiny ol' garage out back, too small for a car nowadays but okay for storing stuff. The whole place come down though the family to his momma, and she left it to him. Being so handy, Mitch kept that house up real good. New paint when it needed some and quick to fix anything broke.

Found him propped up on the couch with an empty six pack on the floor and another beer in hand.

"Come on in, Cuz, and sit by me." His voice was kinda slurry, and I didn't know if it was the beer or the empty pill bottle I spied down between the couch cushions. He picked up the remote and turned down the soap opera he been watching. Pained me to see a grown man drinking beer, watching the soaps and emptying a pill bottle.

"How you doing?" I said. "Back any better?"

"Hell no, and that doctor won't give me another 'scription for my pills. Says I take too many as it is." Mitch winked. "But I found me another way."

That give me a start. "What other way? What're you doing, Mitch? Don't do nothing foolish."

"Not foolish," he said, "just found somebody else to get me some pills." He patted my arm. "Nuff about me. My sister brought by that deer meat, all butchered and wrapped up tight for the freezer. Want you to go out to the garage and take half when you head on home."

I didn't feel right about taking that meat, him being laid up and maybe hooked on pain pills, but I knew Mom was gonna need some soon. Besides, I didn't want to hurt his feelings neither, so I said I'd pick it up at the end of the day so it'd stay frozen.

I tried to get him to talk more about them pills, but he wasn't having any. So I ended up telling him what happened out at Miz Simmons'.

"Goddam. You gotta do something about that. Get yourself a gun and keep it handy." I started to shake my head. "Jimmy Lee," he said, "Okay, you ain't the best shot. Nobody in your branch of the family's much good with a gun. Men all been too busy working the farm, mining coal and taking care of the women and kids. But Junior's out to kill you, and you gotta make sure he don't."

18

WHEN I COME OUTTA MITCH's, the sun finally peeked from behind the clouds for the first time in days. Felt good just to have that warmth on my face, even if the temperature was still near to freezing. Pastor Bob drove by, waved and pulled over to the curb.

"Haven't had one of our talks in a long time," he said. "How about you get in and we go for a cup of coffee?" He smiled. "Bring you back to get your truck after." Well, what was I gonna do? Couldn't say no to the man who been such a force in my life.

On the ride over to the Corner Cafe, I was feeling nervous and guilty. But next thing I knew, we was in the farthest booth, and I was telling everything I been holding back. He made it so easy, I felt my shoulders relax from the knots I didn't even know been there.

He listened to my whole tale, asked a few questions and give me the same advice everybody else been saying about not jumping to conclusions. His eyebrows went up in a question. "You gonna tell the Sheriff what happened out there?"

Felt the corners of my mouth turning down. "Sheriff thinks I mighta killed Miz Simmons, so I try to keep outta his way. Don't wanna talk to him about nothing."

Pastor Bob smiled, to soften his words I thought. "Well, you might want to think that over. Telling Sheriff Price what happened might help your case."

He patted my arm. "Let go and let God," he said.

We was silent a while, and that's what I tried to do, let God be in charge of my life. I come to feel lightened, like Pastor Bob took my load and give it up to the Lord. I just set there, letting that good feeling wash through me.

Then he said, "What if you prepare a lesson and lead the junior high kids at Sunday School?"

I didn't know what to make of that. "This some kinda punishment?" I said. "For holding back all this time?"

He smiled. "Nope. Been thinking about this quite a while. Good chance for you to see if you got the Call."

I was filled with awe just to think of it. "Don't know if I could manage to do it every week."

"Not talking about every week. Just one Sunday. Give it a try and see if it works out."

"You really think I could do that?"

"Wouldn't have mentioned it if I didn't."

"I sure would need some help."

Another one of his kindly smiles. "What I'm here for. Think about it, okay?" He stood. "Come on, let's get you back to your truck and us on with our day."

I remembered it was my turn to visit Bethanne again, so I got a quick bite at the hospital cafeteria and went on up to her room. The woman who'd been in the first bed was gone, and another one was in her place, moaning just under her breath. Bethanne was still there, what with being hurt so bad. But the bruises on her face was turning kinda yellow, and her eye was starting to open.

I pulled the curtain between the beds and took the hand that wasn't in a cast. "You're starting to look a little better. Anything I can do for you?"

She looked up, give me as much of a smile as her face would allow and said, "Get me a Coke, Jimmy Lee. All they'll let me have is water, and I'm sick to death of it."

So I snuck down the hall to the machine, got her a cold Coke and snuck the can back in the pocket of my new jacket. Poured some into the empty glass and held it with the straw so she could take a sip.

"Mmmmm-mmmm. That's the best thing happened in days." She leaned back and give me a good look. "What's been happening with you?"

There I was again, telling my tale and getting pretty darn sick of the telling too.

"Sure it was Junior?" she said.

"You been talking to Eden? You two sound just alike."

"Haven't heard a thing from Eden about this. But you didn't see who it was, did you?"

Had to admit to the truth of that, and she said, "So who else could it have been?" Then I had to go over the others, Orrin Dent and Hank Conner.

"I'm not saying it's not Junior," she said. "God knows he's acting guilty enough about Miz Simmons. But you been snooping around a lot, tricking Orrin into telling you stuff he might not wanna say, following a bank president home. Any chance Conner saw you in his rearview mirror?"

I shrugged to say I didn't know, but her words set me to wondering if my old truck did stand out more'n I thought.

Bethanne wasn't through giving me things to think about. "If I was you," she said, "I wouldn't put all my eggs in one basket just yet."

That made me realize that maybe the Lord was trying to talk to me, like Pastor Bob said. If more'n one person was telling me to think about who else might be the bad guy, I oughta at least check it out. Told Dedianne I'd give Orrin Dent and Hank Conner another look and changed the subject to something less upsetting.

I went to pick up Eden after school, and we both avoided any talk about Junior or anything else connected to Miz Simmons and Lazarus. We wasn't exactly back the way we was, but we was trying.

Rounded off the day picking up that deer meat from Mitch. It was all dressed and packaged, so all I had to do was take it home and put it in the deep freeze out on the back porch. Dad enclosed that a long time before, so we could put a lotta stuff out there. No heat or insulation, but there was a couple outlets, and we could plug in whatever we needed. Mom ironed out there in the summer. Cooler than in the house, 'cause she could open all the windows and have a cross breeze. Anyway, I put the deer meat away and went in to get Mom so she could take a look. She smiled. "That Mitch is more'n a nephew and cousin to us," she said. "We'll save this for when we need it."

The next morning, I got a call from Sheriff Price asking me to come by that afternoon at two. Spent the rest of the day working on the farm and wondering what the heck he wanted. Just thinking about it made me all prickly. Eden and Pastor Bob been coaxing me to tell him about being shot at, but that was my business, not his. At least for now.

Had no idea how long the Sheriff was gonna keep me, so I phoned Eden and told her I'd be tied up and couldn't drive her home from school, like I done recently. She was so okay with that, it set me to puzzling what was happening with us.

Anyway, after lunch I got cleaned up and drove into town. That one sunny, cold day was over, and the gray skies was back. But it was warmer, somewhere round forty or even forty-five. Just like before, the Sheriff kept me waiting in the outer office long enough to get me fidgety. Once I was standing in front of his desk, he leaned way back on his chair's spring, looked at me through squinted eyes, and smiled his nasty smile with the gold tooth showing at the back. "What's this I hear about you being out to Miz Simmons' place?"

I was completely flabbergasted, but I wasn't gonna let him see that. "Who told you?"

He lit up a cigar. "Oh, a little bird from around there."

Junior. Nobody else lived up there. That son-of-a-gun couldn't get me with a rifle, so he was gonna get me tattling to the Sheriff.

"Junior tell you he shot at me too?"

The Sheriff flew upright in his chair. "Shot at you? What're you talking about? You making up stories, Jimmy Lee? Trying to make me look the other way?"

I was still standing there, my mind whirling round and round, trying to get a hold on everything whipping by so fast. But I already mentioned being shot at, so I had to go on with it. Knew I had to be careful though.

I reached for the old wood chair off to the side of his desk and set down. "Yeah, I was there Monday. Just looking round. It's gonna be my place after all, and I was figuring out what I was gonna do with it."

Lord, that's a white lie, I prayed, and You know why I'm

telling it. Once all this is done, I'll do whatever You ask of me.

I leaned forward, wanting the Sheriff to see the truth. "Somebody took a couple shots at me. Dunno, maybe they thought I was a deer?"

He leaned toward me too, put his arms on his desk and let the smoke of his cigar swirl up to the ceiling. "I'm not talking about Monday. Orrin Dent told me you was out there stirring up the ashes a while back. What was you looking for?"

Orrin. Not Junior. Things was still whipping by too fast for me to keep track. Took a big swallow and put my mind back to me moving ashes. "Oh, that. I went out to get some of them ashes and put 'em beside where Miz Simmons and me put her dog's ashes. Figured some of that had to be her, and she'd wanna be with Lazarus."

"Jimmy Lee, you sure can tell a tall tale when you want to."

"Swear to God, Sheriff, that's the truth. I went out there to sprinkle some of Miz Simmons' ashes with her dog's." Sounded pretty dumb, the way I told it. Held my breath and waited while he took a long draw on that cigar.

He squinted through the smoke. "And what's this about you getting shot at Monday?"

"Maybe hard to believe, but somebody shot at me. Twice."

"Was that before or after you tried to run Hank Conner off the road?"

"What?" This time I swallowed so hard I almost choked. "He nearly run *me* off the road. Come uphill so fast, I had to steer to the berm and pray to the Lord."

"You're big on calling on the Lord. That how you hide the truth?"

Felt like no matter what I said, Jerry Price found a way to twist it round. What was I gonna do? Took a big breath and let it out slow. "Sheriff, I don't know what else to tell you. What I said was the God's truth, even it don't ring true to you. I ain't got no proof here, but you can go out and see for yourself. We can go together, and I'll show you where one of them bullets hit the rock I was standing by."

He stubbed out his cigar. "Maybe we'll just do that. No time like the present."

19

So WE DROVE ON OUT TO MIZ Simmons' place. Sheriff wanted us both to go in his car, but I said I needed to get home right quick after we was out there, so he let me drive myself. But he made me go in front and followed so close on my bumper, I thought he might end up in the truck bed. Don't think I ever drove that safe before or since.

I led the Sheriff round behind the burned ruins and pointed up the hill. "That's where it was, right up there. Took two shots at me."

Sheriff give me a funny look. "How come you was up there?"

I gulped and hoped it didn't show. Didn't wanna tell him about looking for clues, 'cause he'd say it wasn't my place to do that. So I said, "Lotta water comes down off of that ridge. Me and Miz Simmons was talking about maybe putting in a ditch to make it go where it'd do the most good. I was up there trying to see what might work."

He looked at me like he might believe that when pigs fly, but he waved me toward the hill. "Come on. Show me what you got to show me."

We hauled ourselves up there. The gouge where the bullet hit the rock was plain as day. "That's it, Sheriff. That's where the first one hit."

He rubbed a dirty-nailed thumb in the gouge. "Where's the other one?"

"On down the hill. I jumped for cover behind one of them trees."

"Which one?"

And it hit me I didn't know. Which one was it? "Not real sure, 'cause I was jumping for my life, but I know it was big enough for me to hide behind."

We started down toward where the cabin used to be, looking at every tree it mighta been, but we couldn't find the right one.

The Sheriff stopped and held up a hand. "Jimmy Lee, that rock could've been gouged by a lot of things, including you using a hammer to make a good story."

I gulped for sure then, and he musta seen it, 'cause he said. "Find me that tree with the bullet in it, or I don't know what to believe."

"Let me start over," I said. "Let me try to jump and hide like I done then."

He kinda moved back and pulled his arm out like he was saying go ahead. So I climbed up to the rock again and went through the motions I remembered. Bent down and looked at that little hole underneath the ledge where a fox mighta gone. Saw the gouge where the bullet hit the tobacco and sent it flying. Then I remembered something so important I don't know how I come to forget it.

"Sheriff, there was three shots. One of 'em whizzed by my ear, and that's what caused me to jump."

And jump I did, away from that whizzing sound and as far down the hill as I could. Straight down, not down toward the cabin where we been looking. I slammed into that big ol' tree and held on like I done before, 'cause I knew this was truly the one. Sure enough, when we climbed round to the other side, there was a hole right where my heart woulda been if I was standing there.

But it wasn't a bullet hole. Somebody'd used a knife to dig out whatever been inside. Lord, I thought, help me now.

Sheriff put his finger in that hole and felt inside so long, I thought I was gonna die from holding my breath.

"I believe you, Jimmy Lee," he said, and I sucked in enough air near to make me light-headed. "Somebody shot at you, and I'm going to get my deputies over to the other side of the holler and look for shell casings."

I musta broke into a grin, 'cause he said, "Don't get your hopes up. Anybody smart enough to dig a bullet out of a tree is smart enough to police his casings."

Near dark when I got home, winter nights come on so early. All the way, I was thanking the Lord that the Sheriff was starting to believe me. Just kinda sang it to myself, "Praise the Lord. Praise the Lord." But underneath was the fret Junior tried to kill me, and what was I gonna do about it? How was I gonna protect myself 'til Junior was brought to trial? That could take weeks, maybe months, maybe never if me or the Sheriff didn't find the proof. Meanwhile, I had to do something.

After supper, when the kids was all in bed, I told Mom I needed a gun.

She looked up from sewing on a button. "Wondered when you might be thinking about that." She put down her handwork and said, "Come on, then."

The guns was always kept in her and Dad's bedroom, even the .22 Dad give me when I was fourteen. Us kids hardly never went in there. That was their special place. When Dad was alive, he got the rifles and brought 'em downstairs for us to use when we went hunting. Which wasn't often. After he passed, that one time I was going hunting with Mitch, I paid Mom the courtesy of asking her to bring down Dad's .30-30 Winchester. Didn't want to trespass on the room that maybe held her sorrow.

But this night was differnt. Mom motioned me to follow her upstairs to the bedroom. I was right behind and watched her open the closet door. Seemed like the smell of Dad come rushing out, kinda mix of tobacco and honest sweat. Felt like that room held my sorrow too. But course it was my imagination, and I put a tight grip on that, so my mind wouldn't go wandering to all the things he been to me.

Mom reached way back into a dark corner of the closet and brought out a canvas gun case. "Here," she said, holding it out. "Better take the shotgun. Load of buckshot'll bring down just about anything."

I unzipped the case, and she stood on tiptoe to reach down an old shoebox. I opened it up, and there was two boxes of shells inside, double-ought and number four squirrel shot. "Use the double-ought," she said. "Best if you gotta shoot at something big." She smiled up at me, but her smile was small and sad. "Now you know where everything is, case you need the rifle too."

I brought the shotgun and shells back down to the sofa. Mom settled into her chair and picked up her sewing. I spent the rest of the evening cleaning Dad's single shot twelve-gauge, making sure everything worked right. Then I carried it out to the truck and put in the rack behind the seat with the box of shells handy. Took care to make sure the truck was locked safe and went back inside.

Mitch was right. I wasn't any better shot than Dad was, but

least I'd feel safer. Maybe word'd get round about that shotgun, and Junior'd think twice about shooting at me again.

I woke up the next day thinking about going by the Sheriff's office to see what they mighta found across the holler where the shooter was, but something told me to just lay low. Keep outta Sheriff Price's way and let him come to me when he had something. Don't push it, Jimmy Lee, I said to myself and knew it was good advice.

Them thoughts brought to mind what he said about Orrin Dent and Hank Conner telling him stuff about me. Was they trying to get their own stories in before I could say anything? Why would Orrin even bother to talk to Sheriff Price at all? You'd think that pot-grower'd wanna lie low even more'n me. Why tell the Sheriff about me stirring up ashes out at the cabin unless he been the one been doing that hisself? But what might Orrin been looking for?

I come back to the thought that maybe Conner did have a reason to search in them ashes. Maybe he was trying to find any proof Miz Simmons had of him cheating her family. Maybe he thought she hid it in a safe that survived the fire, buried under what little bit of rubble was left. He probably had a safe in his mansion and thought she had one too. Then he found me coming down the hill toward her place. He knew I helped her rebuild that cabin, so maybe I knew where the safe was. That could be reason to stop me from finding what he couldn't.

Well, them thoughts about Orrin Dent and Hank Conner seemed a little far-fetched, but I decided to keep 'em in mind. Folks I trusted kept telling me not to focus just on Junior. Maybe there really was three suspects, and I was so in love with the idea of Junior doing everything that I was blind to the other two.

Mulling over all them thoughts made me realize it was time for another meet in the backroom of Gifts-n-Such. Time for everybody to say what was new and work out the next plan. But Bethanne was still in the hospital. Could we meet there? Nah, that was stupid. Talk about such things with another woman laying in the next bed? Nope, it had to be the back room of the shop. But how long would that take? I needed to talk with Eden in the worst way, and not just about what was happening with us. So I called her right then to say I'd pick her up after school.

20

GOT UP AND GOT BUSY TAKING care of chores round the farm. Miz Monroe called to say Mr. Farnsworth had finished writing up something so I could make clear what I wanted since I was too young to have a will. I told her I was coming to town that afternoon anyway, and we fixed it up that I'd come by to sign that paper round 2:30. And that's what I done, signed it, thanked Mr. Farnsworth and left feeling no matter what, he would always be there for me.

Drove over to Lewiston High just as classes were getting out. When Eden got in the truck, I asked if she had time for a hot chocolate at the Quik Treet before she had to be home. We ended up parked out back, drinking our cocoa and having us a long-overdo heart-to-heart. But not exactly like I planned.

"Jimmy Lee," she said, her face so serious I thought her eyes might shoot lightning into me any minute. "How come you're carrying a shotgun in this truck?"

"Mom give it to me for protection after I been shot at." I smiled, hoping to soften her some. "Not planning to use it. Just want it seen so the word gets out not to mess with me."

Her face filled with scorn to match her voice. "And you think that'll be enough? Just 'cause you're carrying a gun?"

I kept on trying to keep the peace and smiled again. "Well, it might help. Couldn't hurt."

"Oh yes it could," she said. "You might get hurt. Or you might hurt somebody." She shook her head. "Either way, it's no good."

I tried one more time. "I hear what you're saying, and I'm gonna give it some careful thought. Okay?"

She didn't look too happy, but she said, "Okay."

I changed the subject right then and there. "You been giving me some good advice, and I'm gonna take it. You're right, maybe it wasn't Junior shot at me." And I told her what the Sheriff said about Orrin and Conner trying to get me in trouble and how that made me think more about one of 'em being the bad guy.

She started nodding her head, and I knew I was on the right track. For us, at least. "Seems like we need another meet with Mae and Bethanne," I said. "Need to tell each other what we know and make a plan to find out what we don't know."

I could see she was thinking about it, and I wanted her to see I'd thought about it too. "But that might take a while with Bethanne in the hospital," I finished up.

Eden reached out and touched my arm. "That's a relief. You're finally looking at the bigger picture like we all been telling you for some time." She smiled. "Bethanne's gonna be let outta the hospital tomorrow."

She counted the days off on her fingers. "That's Friday, probably afternoon, by the time she gets home. So let's give her Saturday and Sunday to rest up and see if we could meet in her apartment with Mae on Monday. How's that sound?"

Sounded so good, I took her hand and held on tight. "Best news I've had in a long time. Bethanne going home and us being a team again."

I started grinning, but she come back with a damper. "Wait a minute. When did Sheriff Price tell you about Hank Conner and Orrin Dent? What's been going on?"

So I had to tell her about the Sheriff calling me in and us two going out to Miz Simmons' place and the search we made.

She set there real quiet for a spell, twisting her heart-bracelet round her wrist. "Okay. Maybe the Sheriff's starting to trust you. But you need to ask him if his men found anything. We got to know that before we meet." She looked at the time on her cell phone. "Lordy, I need to be getting on home."

We drove over to the trailer park, listening to Scotty McCreery sing "I Love You This Big" on the radio and holding hands. Felt like that was our song.

I parked in front of her trailer and decided it was now or never. "What's happening with us?"

Eden took her hand back and clutched both together in her lap. "What d'you mean?"

I looked at her staring out the window and not at me. I said, "Seems like we been outta sorts a lot lately."

She took in a big breath and let it all out. Then she turned to face me. "We both been under a lotta stress. Bethanne getting beat up, you getting shot at. Not to mention your losing Miz Simmons in such a horrible way. And your dad too." She patted my hand but didn't hold it. "Let's get through this and see where we are."

Eden give me a little peck on the cheek and got outta the truck. Then she turned back. "You don't need to drive me to school tomorrow. Momma wants me to do some things for her first. I can find my own way." I set there, learning how I had to be satisfied with what I got.

Next morning, after the farm chores, I drove into Lewiston and up to the Sheriff's. Had to set round as usual in the waiting room for a spell, but then I got shown into his office.

"Take a seat, Jimmy Lee," he said, and I figured that was an improvement over the last times I been in his office. He smiled, "You here about what we found across the holler where somebody shot at you?"

I nodded and started to ask, but he cut me off with a wave of the hand. "Just like I thought," he said. "Nada. Nothing. Two of my deputies combed that whole hillside, and there wasn't a bullet casing to be found. Like I said, anybody smart enough to dig a bullet out of a tree gonna be smart enough to pick up his brass."

Well that was that, I thought and started to say thank you and get up. But he cut me off again. "Hang on, hang on. They did find the imprint of a knee and a foot where somebody probably knelt to steady the rifle. Somebody shot at you for sure. The prints were all messed up in the muddy ground, though, so no way to make a useful cast."

I set my bum back down and waited to see if there was gonna be any more, and sure enough, there was.

Sheriff Price leaned forward, both elbows on the desk. His face had this look that said I-mean-it-so-pay-attention. "Now just because I believe you doesn't mean you can go off conducting your own investigation like I been hearing. I want this to stop, here and now. You're not to search for anything or follow anyone or do anything else you might think of that helps you be a detective. You leave the detecting to me and my deputies."

He lifted his head. "Are we clear? You understand what I'm saying?"

I nodded. "Yessir, I sure understand." Then I got up and left too quick for him to ask if I was gonna do what I understood.

Decided it was time to go see Mitch again and found him just the same as last time—laying on the couch, watching the TV, drinking beer and dropping pills.

"You want a beer, Jimmy Lee?" he asked. "Oops. Sorry, forgot you don't drink. Help yourself to a Coke from the fridge."

So I did that, come back, and set down in the worn old chair next to him. He wasn't as far gone as before, so I had some hope we might be able to have us a real talk. Shied away from bringing up what he was doing to hisself. Maybe later, I thought, after we talked about other things.

Popped the top on the Coke and said, "Don't I remember you and Orrin Dent worked on some construction sites together?"

He lit a smoke. "Yeah. Why?"

"You know I been shot at." He nodded, and I said. "Well, I found out Orrin Dent was telling tales about me to the Sheriff. Why you figure he'd go and do that?"

Mitch set up like he was grabbed by something important. "I never told you and Miz Simmons this before, but Orrin purely hated that dog. Woulda killed Lazarus hisself if Junior hadn't beat him to it."

"But that's no reason to come after me."

He took a pull on his cigarette. "You been doing anything to put pressure on him? Orrin hates to be pressured about anything. Even knocked down the job boss once 'cause he thought the man been pressuring him to work faster than was safe." Mitch shook his head. "Orrin got kicked off the site, but I guess he figured it was worth it."

I thought back to me pretending to have a flat tire and asking

Orrin for help while I pushed him to talk about Miz Simmons and Lazarus and Junior. "Yeah, I did awhile back, but it didn't amount to much."

"It don't need to amount to much," Mitch said. "Orrin can't abide being pushed by nobody about nothing. You probably riled him without knowing it."

"Guess I must've," I said and remembered Orrin saying Miz Simmons was a good woman but she shoulda done more to control her dog. Had he felt so pushed he had to punish her? Just how long did he carry a grudge? If he knocked down a job boss, would he fire her house? Seemed just as far-fetched as the last thoughts I had about Orrin, but he sure been acting strange.

Mitch downed a couple pills outta a plastic baggie with a gulp of beer, and that give me the opening I was waiting for.

I tried to keep my voice gentle. "Worried about you taking all them pills."

He stubbed out his cigarette. "They *are* getting to me. Seems like I need more and more, and they do less and less."

I leaned forward and looked him in the eye. "Maybe you need help getting off them pills and back to your old life."

He smiled like he didn't mean it and shook his head. "Ain't nothing nobody can do for me."

"Think maybe I know somebody could help. What if I just talk to him without naming names?"

"J.L., you can talk all you want, but it ain't gonna help."

I took that as the okay I needed and got up to go. Give Mitch a pat on the shoulder when I passed. He looked up like a man who'd lost hope a long time ago.

21

SPENT ALL DAY SATURDAY DOING chores round the farm, the older kids helping where they could. I was trying to let go of my troubles and focus on the work, but it didn't help much. Mom fixed us a nice supper of chicken and dumplings with green beans and tomatoes she canned last summer.

After the kids was all in bed, I set up with Mom. She was doing mending like she always done in the evening, and I was holding my Grammy's King James Bible. I breathed a little prayer, told the Lord how I was feeling put upon and needed help. Then I let the Bible fall open, and what come up but Psalm 121. I always think the Lord had West Virginia in mind when he give David the idea to write that Psalm.

"I will lift up mine eyes unto the hills, from whence cometh my help. My help cometh from the Lord, which made heaven and earth."

I read it all the way through, paying careful attention, right up to them comforting last words. "The Lord shall preserve thy going out and thy coming in from this time forth, and even for evermore."

I closed my eyes and let my thoughts roam through that Psalm, repeating it from memory, 'cause I learned it by heart long, long ago.

"The Lord shall preserve thee from all evil: He shall preserve thy soul."

And it come to me that my faith had got weak. The Lord had a plan for me. He wasn't gonna let me get shot. He was gonna help me find Miz Simmons' killer. And He was gonna watch over me forever. I just had to put my trust in Him, and all would be well. Even if He didn't lead me where I thought I wanted to go. That was the hard part. I had to try not to lead the Lord and let Him lead me.

I opened my eyes and saw Mom watching me. "Lord speaking to you?" she asked.

"Yes ma'am," I said, "He sure is."

Then I realized there was more to it than I thought. That Bible didn't open to Psalm 121 just for me. It also opened for them kids the Lord wanted me to teach in Sunday School. I had my scripture. Now I had to find the lesson that would reach 'em as it reached me.

Went to bed feeling more peaceful than in all the time since me and Miz Simmons and Lazarus spent our happy days together.

Woke up the next morning raring to go to church. Put everybody in the old station wagon been in our family for years and drove so fast Mom give me a look. I slowed down to the speed limit and tried to ponder the moral of that look. She kept her eyes shifting between me and the speedometer the whole way.

Got there a little early and waved at Eden, just coming on foot with her momma. Spoke nice to Miz Jones like I been taught and followed Eden's high sign over to the edge of the parking lot. The sun was shining again after a bunch of gray days, and her eyes was just as bright.

"Meeting's set for Monday after school," she said. "Upstairs, in Bethanne's apartment over the shop. Big Jim'll be there too."

"How come?"

"Dunno. Mae just said he's coming. We have to be satisfied 'til we find out on Monday."

Then it was time to go in for Bible Study before Services, and I turned my mind to that. But it wasn't easy.

After church, I held back to be the last one to talk with Pastor Bob while he shook hands at the door.

"Jimmy Lee, you look like you've surely been blessed on this glorious day."

"Yessir, that's the truth. I feel blessed 'cause my faith has been strengthened, and I found the scripture for my Sunday School lesson."

His smile seemed to fill his whole face. "So you're going to do it?" I nodded my head, and he put a hand on my shoulder. "What's the text?"

"Psalm 121. I will lift up mine eyes unto the hills."

"I've always liked that one myself," he said. His smile this time was more of a grin. "But maybe you better use the Modern English Version for those junior high kids."

I smiled back. "Yeah. I been thinking that too." Then I remembered I wanted to talk about Mitch, and the smile left my face. "Pastor Bob, my cousin's got hooked on painkillers. Every Sunday, you always make an announcement about the AA Meeting. He's drinking a lot too. Can I come talk to you about getting him some help?"

Outta the corner of my eye, I could see Mom standing by the car door, the kids inside, and everybody ready to go. Pastor Bob followed my gaze and said, "Sure. Why don't you come by tomorrow, and we'll talk about how our Meetings might help."

Figured the best time to go see Pastor Bob was in the afternoon before I picked up Eden from school and went on to our meet at Bethanne's. So I called him Monday morning, and he said two o'clock would suit him fine.

Just like always, he welcomed me into the warm glow of his tiny office. No wonder it's called the Church of the Holy Light. Seems like every time I'm in Pastor Bob's office, that holy light is shining right through the window behind his desk.

I didn't wanna start off talking about Mitch, so I brought up the lesson I was preparing for Sunday School. Asked if I could borrow a Modern English Bible, and Pastor Bob took one right outta his bookcase and give it to me. "Keep it as long as you like." He smiled. "We have lots more."

Then he got real earnest. "Tell me more about what you're going to do with that text."

"I wanna talk about how the Psalm reminds folks in West Virginia that we have proof of the Lord's love and protection all round us. All we gotta do is look up at the hills, and there it is."

He leaned back in his chair. "Good lesson. But don't do all the talking. Be sure and ask the kids questions so they get drawn into thinking it through for themselves."

I hadn't thought about asking questions, but I realized that's how Pastor Bob taught us. He didn't tell us, he helped us find revelations ourselves. But I was stumped about what to ask. "Like what?" I said.

"Like asking the kids if they ever feel close to the Lord when they go up into the hills. Ask 'em to talk about it."

"OK. I think I got the idea." But I knew I just had the idea. I didn't really know what more to ask. This was gonna be harder than I thought. "Let me work on it some and then come see you again?"

"Sure," he said and changed the subject. "Wanna talk about helping your cousin?"

Now I was the one being earnest. "I'm real worried about Mitch. He was a hard worker, always friendly and helpful. Then he fell off a ladder at a construction site and hurt his back. Doc put him on painkillers, but Mitch got hooked and wanted more and more. Now the doc won't give him no more, and Mitch started buying them pills in baggies from God-knows-who. He pops 'em like candy and washes 'em down with beer."

Pastor Bob leaned on his desk. " I noticed Mitch hasn't been in church for a while. When did all this start? How long has he been taking these pills?"

"Not sure exactly. A few weeks maybe."

"So it's not likely he's OD'd?"

Felt like somebody hit me in the heart with a sledge hammer, but I took a deep breath and said, "Word'd get round the family if that happened."

"You said he washes the pills down with beer. Does he have a drinking problem too?"

"Well, he's sure putting down the six packs. Dunno about the hard stuff."

Pastor Bob set back in his chair and smiled. "Is this you wanting to help, or is he asking for help?"

I had to think about it for a second before I said, "I brought it up, and he admitted he was in trouble. Said nobody could help." Pastor Bob started to speak, but I rushed on. "I asked if I could talk to you about it, and he said I could."

Pastor Bob put his elbows on his chair arms and rested his mouth against his clasped hands. His eyes seemed to roam there and there, following his thoughts. Finally he said, "All this isn't as simple as it sounds. Such a short time, maybe Mitch isn't really addicted yet. But he's surely dependent on those painkillers. His body wants more and more. He could easily end up addicted. But addicted or dependent, the person has to want help. Sometimes they have to fall pretty far before they'll admit to that. Doesn't sound like Mitch is ready."

My feelings sunk through the floor. "So what should I do? Wait 'til he winds up OD'd in the hospital?"

Pastor Bob got up and walked round his desk. Then he set in the other chair visitors usually take. "We both need to do some praying on this. Your cousin has to *want* to come. If and when that happens, he'll be welcomed with open arms. But don't drag him, because it just won't work."

I was feeling hurt and let down by the man who always held me up. "How do you know?"

He give me this look, somehow sad and warm at the same time. "Because I'm an alcoholic myself."

22

I LEFT THE CHURCH, MY HEAD in a whirl. Pastor Bob an alcoholic? He'd explained you had to admit to yourself that's what you were and fight it everyday, one day at a time. Said he hadn't had a drink in fifteen years. That's what brought him to the Lord, admitting that he couldn't do it on his own. All this was really more'n I could take in, but I had to pick up Eden and get over to Bethanne's on the double. Pushed all that into the back of my mind and tried to concentrate on the things we needed to talk about.

We found Bethanne outta bed and laying on the couch with this crocheted blanket over her. Somebody musta used all the leftover yarn they had, 'cause that Afghan had every color in the rainbow and then some. Anyway, Bethanne was looking lots better'n the last time I saw her in the hospital. Color in her face was almost normal, and she could talk without wincing. Her arm was still in a cast, but hopefully that'd come off before too many more weeks.

Mae'd outdone herself in the baking department. Brought banana bread *and* oatmeal cookies. We all just set there eating that good food, drinking coffee or tea and taking pleasure in being together again with Bethanne home.

We finished our celebration, and Eden helped Mae put the dishes and such in a basket to be cleaned at Mae's house. The leftovers was stashed in plastic tubs for Bethanne to enjoy later. And we each got a glass of water to wet our whistles while we talked.

Mae settled her large frame into a chair beside Big Jim's and said, "Okay, a lot's been happening, and I expect everyone has something to say. Jimmy Lee, you first."

I didn't feel no grudge against her for acting like the leader of our meet. She was probably most removed from what was going on, so maybe she was least emotional. I knew I was filled with feelings after talking with Pastor Bob, and I needed to let go.

I told 'em about Hank Conner nearly running me off the road and me getting shot at. Then I relayed the tales Orrin Dent and Hank Conner told the Sheriff about me. I ended up with Mitch saying Orrin knocked a job boss down, 'cause he felt hisself being pushed round. And telling all this, I realized I was just plain mad. Mad at all them men who wanted to do me harm. What'd I ever done to them?

Bethanne's voice pulled me back from them thoughts. "You ever push Orrin around?" So I had to tell about having a phony flat tire and getting Orrin to help while I pumped him with all kinda questions.

"Enough for him to want to shoot you?" she asked.

"Not enough for a regular person, but him, maybe," I said. Admitting that made me see I *was* doing harm to them men. I had to own up to it and take the results. My life was never gonna be the same 'til all this was over. And maybe not even then.

I looked over at Eden. She was taking notes to beat the band, just like she always done. But I could tell she was upset I hadn't told her about putting pressure on Orrin right after it happened. And probably just as upset that I done it at all.

Finally they all heard enough from me, and that purely was a relief. Felt like I been in the hot seat, and it was time to cool off.

Mae give me a serious look. "I know we haven't been able to meet because Bethanne was laid up in the hospital, but Jimmy Lee, a lot's been happening that you haven't been telling. And we need to know everything if we're going to help."

I felt the truth of what she was saying and knew I had to do a better job of working with folks who wanted the same thing I wanted. We was together in trying to find out who set that cabin on fire. But I didn't have time to feel shamed, cause she smiled and said, "Okay, let's leave that in the past and learn from it." She put a hefty hand on Big Jim's arm. "I asked Jim to come, because it turns out he's had experience with Hank Conner I didn't know about."

Jim nodded once and said, "This started way back when we were in high school together. Davie Secret was the quarterback of the football team, and I was right guard."

What's all this got to do with now, I wondered, but I had to trust Mae that somehow it did.

Jim went on. "Hank Conner was a wide receiver, and a good one too. Had flypaper for hands, seemed like."

He paused for a drink of water. "We were in the state tournament and had a good chance of winning. Davie threw a pass downfield to another receiver, but it slipped through his hands. Probably nervous. Anyway, back in the huddle, Hank was giving Davie hell, saying he'd been wide open and Davie better pass him the ball next time. Davie shut him down and called the play."

Now I was getting fascinated. Great story, and it showed Hank Conner thought a lot of hisself even in high school. Man that vain might do anything to preserve what he thought was his high and mighty self.

"We lined up," Big Jim said, "I was too busy protecting Davie to see what happened next, but I heard about it in the locker room. The other team put two defenders on Hank, and Davie threw the ball to the guy who dropped it before."

Big Jim grinned. "And he caught it. Ran zigzag through the defenders and almost scored a touchdown." His grin faded. "This huge ape came outta nowhere, blindsided our guy and knocked him out cold. By the time he was taken care of and off the field, we lost our momentum. Had to kick a field goal. That went wide, and we lost the game."

He spread his hands on his huge knees and said, "Hank Conner never forgave Davie Secret for losing the game. Said it was all his fault. He, Hank, could've caught that ball and run it in, if only Davie'd had the guts to thread the needle with that pass."

"And he waited years to punish Davie in the worst way he could," Big Jim continued. "Davie had a son, Davie Junior, who was just as great an athlete as his dad. Kid played Pop Warner football, and Hank Conner's bank was one of the sponsors. The bank promised to pay for all the uniforms, and they did. But not for Davie Junior. Hank said there'd been some mistake in the order, and Davie Junior's uniform was left out. That meant Davie had to sit out a couple opening games. The old uniforms had a different look, so he couldn't wear one of those, and Davie Junior said he didn't want his dad to buy him one 'cause it wasn't fair. Bunch of parents took up a collection and bought him a uniform, but the harm was done. I was one of the coaches. We all knew what Hank'd done, but we couldn't prove it."

Big Jim shook his head. "What kind of man punishes a kid for what his dad didn't do years ago?" He took another drink of water. I was setting close, and I saw a tear run outta Big Jim's eye. He used that hand with the missing fingers to wipe it away and held the drink of water to hide what he was doing.

Bethanne shifted position on the couch, and her face showed some pain. I was reminded she was far from healed, even if she was home from the hospital. The cast on her arm was obvious, but she had to be hurting from the operation to take out her spleen. And there was all the other injuries too. Maybe we couldn't see 'em, but they was there just the same. Anyway, she shifted and spoke up. "So Hank Conner waited years to punish Secret's boy because of something that happened when Conner was in high school. How long would he wait to punish Mrs. Simmons for writing in one of her books about him cheating her family?"

We all set there awhile, realizing Conner coulda done it, coulda set that cabin on fire and killed the woman who treated me like family.

I was almost choking on them thoughts when Mae said, "Let me bring it up to the present. I got some news fits in with what happened to you out at Mrs. Simmons' place."

So she tells us her sister—one works as housekeeper for Hank Conner—this sister saw Conner bring a rifle from his car into the house. He was muttering about "damn kid not knowing when to leave well enough alone." One knee of his trousers was muddy, like he been kneeling down. She was wondering why a bank president'd be hunting in the middle of the week.

I was so shook up, I couldn't breathe for a second, and that's how Bethanne got in ahead of me. "When was this?" she asked.

Mae looked over at me. "The day Jimmy Lee was shot at."

"That son of a bitch!" I couldn't help it. Them words just burst from my mouth before I had time to put a damper on 'em.

Eden's pen slammed down on her notebook, and she looked at me, eyes and mouth full to bursting with disapproval.

I rushed to apologize for cussing. I knew better. Dad or Mom woulda skinned me if they heard me say that.

Big Jim grinned, "Couldn't help but think the same thing myself."

Mae put up both hands. "That's okay, Jimmy Lee. We understand. But all that's in the past too. Let's look to the future. What're we going to do next?"

Big Jim grinned again. "I could beat the son of a...beat him up."

Mae sighed like she was asking the Lord for patience and said. "This is serious. Stop clowning around."

He bit his lips and nodded, but his eyes was sparkling like he still thought it might be a good idea.

Eden finally spoke up. "Mae's right. We gotta put the strong feelings of this behind us and figure out what we're gonna do."

I was still feeling pretty het up, but I could see the wisdom of making a plan together. We didn't have no proof of Conner firing Miz Simmons' cabin. Or even shooting at me, if it come to that. I sure wasn't ready to tell the Sheriff nothing of what we knew. Wanted to solve this all by myself, just like I promised when I knelt beside them ashes.

Bethanne said, "Okay, let's take them one by one. Looks like Conner's now our main suspect.

I was still feeling hot anger run through me. "I'm gonna follow that sucker day and night."

Mae held up a hand. "Hold on. That's way too dangerous. If he shot at you out there, what'd he do if he found you lurking around his house? Besides, my sister's there everyday but Sunday. She can watch him without him knowing."

I musta looked kinda sulky, 'cause Eden said, "You know Mae's right about this too. There's other things you can do that none of us can."

And then I saw it. Whatever happened to the bullet that whizzed by my ear? The shooter dug one outta the tree, and the one that ricocheted was probably too ruined to be any good for evidence. But me and the Sheriff, we never looked for the bullet that made me jump to save my life.

I give Eden a big grin. "You know, you're right. I'm gonna look for the missing bullet."

23

So next day, after running some errands for Mom, I drove out to Miz Simmons' place. Told myself I had to stop thinking of it that way. But I was lost somewhere in-between. It wasn't her place now, but it wasn't mine neither.

I was so deep in thought, I almost missed seeing the fence been cut. Right across from the old lumber track that run up the ridge. I stopped, backed up and had a good look. Sure enough, it was cut, not all the way up to the eight-foot top, but enough for a man to squeeze through. I backed up some more and parked the truck halfway inside some pine trees, so you had to look hard to see it. Didn't know if somebody was near, but if they was, I didn't want 'em seeing what I was up to. I got the shotgun, put some shells in my jacket pockets and went back to the fence.

Climbed through, careful not to trip, and snuck down to the stone wall marking the bottom land, the one we rebuilt from what them Thomassons let fall to ruin. I hunkered down behind that wall, four foot high at least, and peeked over. There was Orrin Dent sifting through the cabin ashes with a framed screen like you use to get rocks outta dirt when you're making a vegetable garden. Watched him for five minutes or more from my hiding place. He'd shovel a load of ashes into the screen, pick it up and shake it good, then look to see what was left inside. Every time, he'd toss out whatever it was and start over.

My first thought was to load a shell in my shotgun, walk over to Orrin and ask him what the heck he thought he was doing. Then I realized it made more sense to wait and see if he found what he was looking for. So I stayed hunkered down, not wanting to kneel on the wet ground. I watched him sift and sift, over and over. But he never found whatever it was.

Just when I thought my legs couldn't take no more, squatted down behind that wall, Orrin shook out the screen, picked up a rifle I hadn't seen before and headed up the holler toward the cut in the fence. Lucky for me, he took a path direct from the ruins, so he didn't see my footprints.

I stayed down so he wouldn't see me, filled with thanks the Lord hadn't let me follow my first idea and come up on Orrin with the shotgun. We mighta had a shootout for sure. Once he was outta sight, I raised up and set on that wall, easing my legs and remembering how there'd been tracks in them ashes the first time I come out to get some and put 'em with Lazarus's. Was that Orrin too? And what in the name of all that was holy was he looking for?

Whatever it was, he hadn't found it, and I wouldn't neither. So I might as well get on with looking for that second bullet come whizzing by my ear. I stood up and realized I missed something. Orrin been carrying a rifle. So maybe he was the one shot at me. The shot'd come from his side of the ridge, where he had his pot field up that old lumber road. Was it his bullet I was trying to find?

Lord have mercy, I thought, and set off at a trot up to the rock where it all started. Then I walked back and forth, trying to figure out where that whizzing bullet mighta gone, scuffing with my toe at the fallen leaves, looking for the glint of metal somewhere in all of winter's mess. But just like Orrin, I never found nothing, and that was one more thing I was gonna have to be satisfied with.

Dad always kept a toolbox with nails and screws and wire in the truck. So I hiked back to where I hid it and drove down to the cut fence. Closed it as best I could 'til I could come back with some new fence and patch it up.

All the while, I was thinking about how I got rebuked by Mae for keeping secret all the stuff been happening. Didn't make sense to call another meet about what Orrin was doing. We just had one the afternoon before. So I settled for calling Mae, asking her to tell Bethanne, and I'd tell Eden when I picked her up from school.

Then I drove on over to Gmart and made the last layaway payment on Mom's comforter. Looked all over for a Christmas present for Eden. Nothing seemed right, maybe 'cause things wasn't exactly right between us. Ended up with a long, red neck scarf. At least it was a Christmas color, and it'd keep her warm in all this cold weather.

I got me a pad of paper too, so I could work on my Sunday School lesson for the kids. Went home and hid the comforter in the barn, along with Eden's scarf, tied up in a big plastic Gmart sack. I climbed way up in the hayloft where Mom never went and put 'em in an old metal trunk been there for years. That way, I didn't have no fear the mice'd get 'em before Christmas come. And that wasn't far away now, less'n three weeks. Needed to start thinking about a tree pretty soon.

After lunch with Mom, I went out and did the usual chores, chopped some wood and mucked out the barn so it'd be clean when we could buy a new cow and calf. Then it was time to go get Eden. She wasn't best pleased by my news of what Orrin was doing that morning. But she was as stumped as I was about what else we could do. We was fresh outta ideas about Fireplug Dent. At least for now. She had to study for a big test, so she run into her trailer soon as we got there. We sure wasn't spending special time together like we used to.

But Eden did add one thing that set me to thinking. She said she called Mae at lunchtime to see how Bethanne was doing. Turned out Eden did that everyday, but I didn't know about it. Anyway, Mae said Bethanne was starting to move round better, pain in her side a lot less, but she didn't have her old spirit back. Then Mae reported her sister had called to say Hank Conner was acting peculiar when he got home yesterday. Like he had something to hide, so he was being careful to act super-normal. That played on my mind, but I didn't know what to make of it.

After all that driving round, I needed gas, so I stopped at the PayLo and then parked the truck round to the side, so it wouldn't be in the way of folks come to buy anything from the mini-mart. I went inside to shoot the breeze with my old boss for a while. We was laughing about some of the crazy things customers try to pull, when Junior drove up with Floyd in their beat-up old truck.

No way I wanted to run into 'em, but I did want to watch 'em. So I excused myself to the men's room while Junior come in to pay. Then I skedaddled out the side door and peeked round the corner. Junior was pumping gas into the truck while Floyd got some gas cans outta the back. Floyd started hollering about how he could pump all by hisself, and Junior let him fill up the cans while he watched. Probably making sure Floyd didn't make a mess of things.

Next thing I knew, Floyd started to singing. Junior looked round and hushed him up quick, but not before I heard them words. "No gasoline this time. Not like before. No gasoline this time."

It was getting late in the day, so no way I could follow 'em home and do a little investigating. Remembered what the Sheriff said about not playing detective, but I already decided to pay that no mind. Remembered what Mae said, but this was something I could do that no one else could. So I made up my mind to get over to Junior's first chance I got, when all four brothers was to home, and listen in to what they had to say. That house was so creaky, I could probably just stand by one of them warped window frames and hear every word.

That evening, I tried to work on my Sunday School lesson for the kids, but I sure was having me a problem. I was okay about making the connection between the Psalm and us living in the hills, where proof of the Lord is all round us. And I understood what Pastor Bob said about getting the kids to talk and discover the lesson for theirselves. But I sure was having trouble thinking of questions to ask. I kept writing questions on the pad of paper I bought at Gmart, crossing out words and lines, crumpling up the paper and tossing it away.

Finally, Mom looked up from her nightly mending and said, "You gonna pick up all that paper once you're done covering the floor?"

I nodded, so downhearted I couldn't talk.

"What's the matter?" she said.

"I dunno, Mom." Felt like I was gonna cry but knew I was too big. "Maybe I don't have the Call after all."

She looked at me for a while, nothing to say. Then she nodded once, like she'd made up her mind about something. "No way I can help you with that. You gotta ask the Lord for guidance." Mom smiled. "And maybe you need to get yourself over to Pastor Bob and have a heart-to-heart." She put down the mending she been doing. "Now let's get to bed and let the Lord give us peace."

24

WOKE UP FEELING EVERYTHING was outta sorts. Couldn't get my Sunday School lesson to work. Me and Eden wasn't having them deep talks like we used to. And there didn't seem any way to help Mitch without him first seeing the light. All he was seeing was that baggie full of pills and the bottom of a beer can. Where was he getting them pills, anyway? I had no idea.

Well, there was something I could do about each of them frets, and do it I would. Got up, got fed, told Mom I was gonna see Pastor Bob like she suggested and hit the road.

All the way to Eden's I was thinking about what I was gonna say. No point in bringing up that "what's happened to us" stuff. Needed to get her talking about something serious. And what better than my Sunday School lesson?

She come outta her trailer looking surprised to see me. Now school was back in session, we usually arranged in advance when I'd pick her up and drive her to or from Lewiston High. But she give me a wave and a smile and got in. Her long hair swinging over her shoulder like to make my heart stop.

But I couldn't let that sidetrack me, so I got right down to it as soon as she closed the door. Let out the clutch and took off. Told her I sure needed her help getting that Sunday School lesson off the ground. Said I wanted to use Psalm 121, and she said that was one of her favorites. That felt good. We was on the same track there. So I talked about how Pastor Bob suggested I ask the kids questions to get 'em thinking, but I was having trouble coming up with any that seemed like they'd work.

"Why Jimmy Lee," she said, "that's the easiest thing in the world." She got out her notebook and started writing. "Let's start with Pastor Bob's first question—Do you ever feel closer to the Lord when you're up in the hills?"

She looked over at me. "Some kids are gonna nod their heads yes or put up their hands to show they've felt that way. So what do you say?"

"I dunno." I was practically tongue-tied. "I guess...maybe... something like...'Anybody wanna tell us how you felt?'...something like that?"

She smiled and wrote that down. "Yep. And if the kids are shy about saying something, what do you do?"

"Give up?" I was joking, but only half.

"No, silly, you call on one of the kids who nodded or held up a hand. You ask that one to say a few words about how it felt. Then what?"

"Ask somebody else to say how it felt to them?"

She wrote that down. "Now you're getting the idea. What comes next?"

I almost howled. "Oh Eden, I don't know. I don't have the first idea how to do this."

She give me a little frown. "You're giving up too quick. Ask them to talk about what made them feel that way. If they don't come up with an answer, mention something, like was it the light coming through the trees, or the birdsong, or the water babbling in the creek."

I sighed, and she did too. Then she started to write down a bunch of stuff for the lesson, like asking how the Lord makes us feel safe and to give an example if anybody had one. Her pen was flying over that page, and I was seeing the old Eden. But a new one too, her mind was way ahead of me, more'n it ever been. Especially about something that was so much a part of my life that I never even thought about it. At least not like she done.

We pulled up to Lewiston High, and she ripped the page outta her notebook, jumped out and tossed it on the seat. "Here, this'll give you something to start with." She smiled. "Let me know what else you think of."

Then she was gone, and I was full of how long it been since we had ourselves a little kiss and a hug. Nothing to do but fold up that page and put it in my shirt pocket.

Drove off, feeling worse'n I had when I got outta bed. Wondering if the rest of my day was gonna be the same. I been planning to go see Mitch, but I didn't know if I was ready for what might be waiting for me at his house. So I took the coward's way out and went to the Corner Cafe for a coffee. Saw some guys I knew and jawed for a spell, just talking about this and that and what we thought about whatever it was. Somehow that took away the ache I been feeling, so I got on with visiting Mitch.

Knocked on his door, but he didn't answer. I was pretty sure he didn't feel good enough to drive, so he had to be there. Hollered his name a couple times, then turned the knob and went on in.

He wasn't on the couch, even though the TV was turned on loud enough to wake the dead. No wonder he didn't hear me. Mitch's house wasn't more'n four rooms—living, kitchen, bedroom and bath. That's where I finally found him, passed out in the bathroom, fully dressed and laying face down in his own vomit.

Have to say seeing and smelling that almost made me puke, but I swallowed hard and got him setting up against the wall, even if he was still on the floor. His legs and arms was all floppy, and he was breathing funny, but he was alive. Wet a dirty towel—that's all I could find—and washed his face.

I kept calling him by name, but he didn't answer. Then I shook him a couple times, but that didn't do no good neither. So I pulled him away from the wall, got behind him, put my arms round his chest and drug him to his old iron bed. Got his smelly clothes off and covered him up with an old quilt that had so many holes there wasn't hardly no stuffing left.

Didn't wanna call EMS if I didn't have to. Didn't wanna embarrass Mitch. I was feeling useless, and I started praying out loud. "Lord, we need your help in the worst way. I done everything I can think of, and I don't know what else to do. Tell me, Lord, tell me what to do. Help me save my cousin and bring him back to the life he once had." Kept saying it over and over, all the while patting Mitch's face. "Help me, Lord, help me."

All of a sudden, Mitch stirred. "Piss off."

I felt like dancing a jig to see him awake. Well, almost awake.

"Stop that damn praying, Jimmy Lee, and get me a drink."

I run out to the kitchen and got him a glass of water. Run back and held it up to his lips. He took a sip and backhanded the glass away. It went spinning across the bed, spilling water the whole way. Fell on the floor but didn't break.

I was there to help, but I was starting to get mad. Maybe Mitch was drunk, but we been like brothers. He had no call to treat me that way. I took a breath and asked the Lord to give me the grace to act like a Christian.

I bent down to pick the glass up, and Mitch said, "Get me a real drink. Get me a whiskey."

I stood up and looked down on him from my full six feet. "I can't do that, Mitch."

He opened his eyes to a squint. "Sure you can. There's a bottle in the cupboard."

"Nope. I'm not gonna do that. I'm not gonna give you a drink of anything with alcohol."

His bloodshot eyes glared at me like he was a bull gonna gore me for sure. "Then I was right the first time. Piss off. Piss off right through the door and don't come back."

On the way out, I saw an empty fifth of Wild Turkey laying under the couch.

I had one more stop to make, and I never needed to see Pastor Bob more. Remembered I failed to set up a time but drove on over to the church anyway, hoping for a piece of good luck on that dreadful day.

First thing I done was go into the sanctuary, get down on my knees and ask the Lord to make me strong. Strong enough to bear whatever I had to bear. Then I asked Him to show me the way forward. In my own life. About Miz Simmons' awful death. With Eden and with Mitch. I musta been there longer'n I thought, 'cause when I looked up, Pastor Bob was standing at the altar, waiting for me.

"Saw you drive up," he said. "When you didn't come in the office, thought you must be in need of some time with the Lord."

I stood up and tried to be strong like I been praying. "You sure got that right. But now I'm in need of time with you. Can you spare me some?"

He come down the aisle. "Always. Come on, we'll sit in my office and talk about whatever you want."

I followed him down the hall, feeling kinda numb. But I barely got my backside on the chair before I started spewing out everything that happened at Mitch's. All my fears and despair. Felt like Mitch was already down so far, nothing was gonna help. Not me, not nothing. I failed my cousin, and he cursed me, told me to leave and never come back.

Pastor Bob set in the other visitor's chair and listened to all my pain, never once cutting in to ask a question or make a point. Finally, when I was done, almost blubbering with the burden of it, he said, "Got something I want you to read." He got up and went over to the bookcase. "The Big Book, written by the man who founded AA. Might help you understand what Mitch has got to go through before he's ready for help."

I leafed through it. "I'm not much of a reader, except for the Bible."

He smiled. "That's okay. Pick up it when you feel like it and see what it has to say. It sure helped me, and I'm hoping it'll help you."

"But I'm not the one doing drugs and drinking booze 'til I pass out."

He kept on smiling. "No. But it might help you get a bigger picture of what it takes to beat addiction." He reached out to touch my arm. "You're not failing Mitch. He's failing himself."

He set back and folded his hands. "Shall we pray some?"

I nodded, and he surprised me, praying for Mitch and not for me. Made me realize how much I was seeing the whole thing from my own standpoint. This wasn't about me. It was about Mitch. And I resolved to read The Big Book, cover to cover, if it took all winter.

We set there for a while, just being quiet. Then I remembered I had something else to talk about. Took the paper Eden wrote outta my pocket and showed it to Pastor Bob. Asked him what he thought about using them ideas for my Sunday School lesson.

He read the whole page with careful attention."These are good questions, Jimmy Lee."

Realized I was ducking my head a little. "Well, they're mostly Eden's ideas. I asked her for help."

He smiled with his mouth, but his eyes seemed sorta thoughtful. "I wondered if that was female writing. Eden's a real smart girl." He paused and leaned back. "I think you're ready to give this a try. How about this Sunday? I'll call the regular teacher and ask Mrs. Christie to introduce you to the Junior High Class. Once she's done that, you just get going with this lesson."

I gasped. "Oh no, I'm not ready. It'll take weeks..."

Pastor Bob laid a hand on my arm and cut me off. "You've been working on this over a week. That's more time than any Sunday School teacher would have. Let's make this a real-world try."

I was shaking my head and scooting back in my chair like I might push myself out the door.

He give me a smile and said, "You'll never be more ready. You got your scripture. You got your questions. Go on, take your best shot."

25

THAT GIVE ME THREE MORE days to get ready, and I felt like I needed twice that many, maybe more. But that's all I got, and I set to work in the evenings after I finished my chores. Reading and re-reading Psalm 121. Modern English Version, so I'd be sure not to stumble over it when I was used to King James.

When Sunday come, should I read it to the kids? Or ask one of the kids to read it to the class? Or maybe have all of 'em read it out loud together? Finally decided all of us reading it made the most sense. Start us off working together instead of separate. Keep me from being the one who knew it all and make me just someone helping us see how the Psalm related to our daily lives.

Then I had to work on the questions some more. They was good questions, I knew that. Eden *was* a smart girl, and Pastor Bob give them questions the thumb's up. But they wasn't exactly my questions. Had to figure out what to do to make 'em mine. Went over and over 'em, changing the words to make 'em my words, the way I talk.

I was writing on my pad of paper Friday night, trying to get all this down in some kinda order that I could follow without being too obvious. As usual, Mom was setting across from me, doing some handwork.

"Jimmy Lee, you're fretting that Sunday School lesson to death. Leave go. Trust in the Lord and go to bed."

So I did. Got cleaned up, got in bed and read The Big Book 'til I fell asleep.

The next morning, I realized Mom was right. My Sunday School lesson was never gonna be any better'n it was. Going at it over and over was just getting me more on edge. Besides, I been neglecting my vow to find out who killed Miz Simmons. With Bethanne and Mitch not able to go out to the Roadhouse, we lost our chance to listen in on what Junior had to say. Well, Junior and all his kin was gonna be home on Saturday, and that give me the chance I needed to sneak up on 'em and see what I could hear after that funny stuff about gasoline at the PayLo.

Figured late afternoon was the best time, when they'd be setting round, all relaxed and yapping away. So I run errands for Mom in the morning and did some chores in the early afternoon. Then I told her I had an idea for what to do with Miz Simmons' place once it was all mine, but I needed to check out whether it would really work or not. Mom was busy with the baby, cleaning him up after he dirtied his diaper for the twelfth time that day. So she just waved me bye, and I took off, wearing my camo jacket, dark jeans and a hoodie pulled up so I'd be nearly invisible against the grays and browns of winter.

It started to rain, cold and gusty. That suited me just fine. For sure they'd all be inside where I wanted 'em to be. Maybe dogs too, if they had any, even if we hadn't seen none when me and Miz Simmons found Lazarus dead on Junior's porch. Anyway, I'd keep an eye out for dogs and deal with 'em if and when I had to. Thinking about dogs coming after me got me a little nervous, but I was still determined to get out there and see what I could learn.

I drove up the same old track and walked to where I could look down on Junior's farm and see what was happening before I snuck in. The trees was all bare, and I had a good look at their house and yard. Sure as anything, both the brothers' cars was there, home from working on the Ohio River. Junior's truck was parked right by the sagging front porch. The Lord sure was smiling on me that day, even if the sun wasn't.

Left my truck where it was and hiked down the ridge, my clothes blending in with the hillside. Had to be hard to see me if I didn't move too fast. And that's what I done. Took my time getting down to the paved road and across it, then through some pine trees that give me good cover. Their house was in the shadow of the ridge, so dusk was starting to creep in, even though it was only four o'clock. The rain stopped, but it was still cold and gusty. Seemed like they wouldn't be coming back outside, especially with dark coming on. Still, that didn't mean there wasn't no dogs, so I kept my eyes and ears alert.

I stood hid aways in the pines, some thirty feet from the side of the house. Water dropped from branches where my body touched 'em, and I tried to focus on what I could see, not what I could feel. Smoke coming outta the chimney and a light shining through the window. That window was grimy, but I could see Junior and his two brothers home for the weekend setting with their feet up on a pot-bellied stove. They was passing round a quart jar and laughing about whatever it was.

I went along further to the right, where I couldn't see 'em so they couldn't see me, and snuck up to the house. All the while looking for dogs, but there wasn't none to see, or hear neither. I edged along the house 'til I was beside the window. The frame was warped all right, but I still couldn't hear what they was laughing at. Cursed myself for being glad it was winter with everybody indoors. Course they was inside with the windows and doors all closed. How was I gonna hear anything?

I hunkered down and looked to the left and right, but there wasn't nothing helpful in sight. Decided I might as well go all round the house in case I could find a window cracked or something, anything that'd help. Expected to find the back door locked, and it was. Still, I felt downhearted when I couldn't open it just enough to hear something. Then I looked down and saw the entrance to the crawl space under the house. That little door was open and beckoning me to come on in. Got the shivers just looking at it.

Now I never told this before, not even to Eden, but I get the willies in tight spaces. Don't know why, just do. Break out in a sweat, and heart starts to thumping like it's gonna break open my chest. Feel like I can't get enough air, like I'm gonna suffocate. So I sure didn't wanna go under that house. But what other choice did I have? Figured them old floorboards had to be as warped as the window frames, so if I got under the Flint brothers, maybe I'd hear every word.

I took a deep breath and blew it all out. Asked the Lord to make me calm, so I could do what I had to do. Then I got down on my knees and crawled inside. Lord have mercy, it was cold and damp under there, cobwebs every which way. Smell of rat turds and the squeak of something as it scurried away. I started to back out and go home. Then I thought of Lazarus dying in his own blood and Miz Simmons burned to death. Knew I had to go on, even if panic tried to hold me back.

My heart was hammering against my ribs so strong, it seemed like I could hear it. Never prayed so hard as I did then. "My help cometh even from the Lord, which made heaven and earth." Kept saying that over and over 'til I felt myself calm some. Then I started crawling toward where I could see a sliver of light shining through the floorboards. Scraped my knee on something hard but kept going 'til I could lay down under that light and listen.

At first, they was teasing Junior about when him and Becky was gonna have another baby. "Not if I can help it," he said, his voice kinda mad. "She fooled one time, but it ain't never gonna happen again."

One of the brothers give a nasty laugh. "So you gonna leave off poking her?"

I heard the legs of a chair hit the floor, and Junior said, "I poke who I want when I want, and it ain't none of your damn business. So shut your trap before I shut it for you."

They was all silent for a while. I was beginning to lose hope, when the other brother said, "At least Becky cured you of them boils."

"She didn't cure me of no boils," Junior said. "That witch burning up is what cured me. The only thing Becky can cure is......." And they all started to laugh like he made some gesture I could only guess at.

Come on, I thought, say more about the fire. Get back to the fire.

Without warning, the chair legs hit the floor again, and Junior called out, "Floyd?" There was a pause, then footsteps coming to the back door, and it banged open. Junior's voice come out twice as strong. "Floyd? Where's that damn wood? Fire's about to go out."

Fear grabbed my throat and squeezed it good, 'cause I heard footsteps outside the cellar door. I forgot all about Floyd. I seen Junior and his two brothers inside, but not Floyd. Floyd was outside, and he was coming closer and closer. I was too scared even to pray. My breath stopped, and I shut my eyes so I could focus on what my ears could hear. The steps come closer. I opened my eyes and looked down the length of my body to where there was a dim light from that little door I crawled through.

There was Floyd's feet, standing right outside and wearing a pair of work boots. All scuffed and muddy, looking like they was gonna fall apart any second. Junior's voice come through the open door. "Floyd, what're you doing out there? Get that wood in here now. And let them dogs out."

"Yes, Junior. Anything you say, Junior. Always do what you say."

The sound of Junior's feet come back to just above me, and Floyd's boot pushed the crawl-space door shut. Then I heard the sound of metal scraping on metal. Floyd had locked me in. I was in a tight place for sure.

26

THOUGHT I WAS GONNA PASS out, what with the door bolted shut and the dogs on the loose. Seemed like there wasn't enough air under that house to keep a mouse alive, let alone a sixteen year-old boy. Worked hard to get my breathing under control again. Long as I was shut under the house, the dogs couldn't get me, so I might as well focus on hearing what I could hear. If I could just keep the panic down. So I laid still under that sliver of light, my ears twitching with the effort.

But all I heard was Floyd's feet crossing the floor and firewood getting dumped beside the stove. Then come the sound of three pairs of work boots heading for the front door.

Floyd's voice was near hysterical. "Where you going, Junior? You mad at me? I done like you said."

Junior answered like he was full outta patience. "Told you we was going to the Roadhouse for beer and burgers, just as soon as you brought in the firewood. You let them dogs out?"

"Yes, Junior, done that too."

"Don't hear 'em."

Floyd got all whiny. "They run off after a rabbit. Don't be mad, Junior. I couldn't help it."

One of the other brothers spoke up, all outta patience hisself. "They'll come back. Let's go, Junior! I'm hungry."

Floyd started to singing, "Beer and burgers. Beer and burgers."

"Get in the car," Junior said.

The front door slammed, and an engine started up. Then come the sound of tires pulling away, followed by dogs baying. Couldn't tell how many dogs they was, but they sure was baying to beat the band. Maybe 'cause they was left behind? Or maybe they wasn't fed yet? If they was baying, they was hunting dogs. That sure didn't ease my mind, hungry hunting dogs standing between me and my truck. What if they was mean, beat up like Lazarus? They'd come for me for sure.

I let out a long sigh. Didn't even know I been holding my breath 'til I did that. This whoosh of air just kept coming out. I needed me a plan, and it had to be a good one. I was locked under the house, and dogs was waiting for me. What the heck was I gonna do?

Sounded like the dogs was at the front of the house. They hadn't come round to the little door Floyd bolted, so that was a good thing. Hard to see under there, but that little door didn't close tight, and there was just the faintest gray light come round it. I started scooching feet first toward that door just as quiet as I could. Didn't want them dogs to hear a thing and come looking for me. Cobwebs kept grabbing my face and hands. My clothes smelled of rat, and that smell was like to choke me, it was that strong. Made myself keep swallowing just to keep that choke down, even though there wasn't much spit to swallow. And all the while, fear held me so tight I thought I might get paralyzed.

Finally my feet come up against the wall by the door, but now I had to figure out what to do. If I kicked the door, the dogs'd hear and come running. Now, I been a friend to dogs all my life, but this was differnt. Them dogs was gonna hurt me bad just as soon as they got the chance. I needed something to make 'em afraid, keep 'em away, and I needed it fast. I didn't wanna hurt 'em if I didn't have to. I laid there and tried to remember if there was anything outside the door I might use. For the life of me, I couldn't remember a thing. Had I seen the wood pile? How far away was it?

I felt in my pockets but all I found was keys, money, some string and my penknife. That penknife didn't have much of a blade. Dogs'd be right on me before I could slash at 'em. That set me to wondering if I could find a stick or something under the house I could use. I felt all round me, but there wasn't nothing to find. I was afraid to get too far from the little door in case I couldn't locate it again.

Outside, I knew it'd be getting darker by the minute. I needed to be able to see to defend myself, so I had to do something and do it quick. I took my penknife and made a little hole between the thin door boards so I could see out. Couldn't see much, but it did let in some light. Then I slipped the knife in the crack between the door and the wall and slid it down 'til it touched the bolt. Made another hole there, so I could see what I was dealing with. Didn't seem like a bolt. It was too thin, like maybe one of them hooks that fastens into an eye screwed into the wall. Maybe that was the metal I heard, a hook going into an eye.

I put my knife under whatever it was and pushed up as hard as I could. But careful, so there wouldn't be much noise and the door wouldn't pop open. All the while, I was listening for them dogs. Maybe they was out at the front, but they had sharp ears. Didn't wanna be in that tight spot with them dogs rushing in to get me. Nothing happened with the little door. If it was a hook and eye, they sure fit tight. I kept pushing that knife, wiggling it up and down and trying to hold onto the door's crossbar so it wouldn't open, my heart beating wild and my ears straining to hear where them dogs was.

And then it happened. The hook slid outta the eye, and the door jumped open a crack. I pulled it back as best I could and tried to figure what to do now. I could get out, but I didn't have nothing to defend myself with. Thought about how lotta folks keep stuff under their houses, stuff that still might be useful. Maybe if I went back to where the light was shining down through the floorboards, I might see something. Didn't wanna leave the unlocked door in case the dogs come, but I didn't see what else I could do.

Once again, I started crawling toward that light. And once again, I scraped my knee on something. Why hadn't I remembered that? Mind too messed up with fear? Anyway, I stopped and felt round in the dirt 'til my hand hit something metal. I felt some more and nearly let out a whoop. It was a length of machine chain, four feet long and a half-inch or so wide, some heft to it. Not perfect, but maybe good enough. Praised the Lord, picked it up and crawled for the little door.

I come through that door arms and head first, swinging the steel chain for all I was worth. Heard them dogs running, baying like they treed a 'coon. But I wasn't about to be up a tree with dogs howling all round. I whirled that chain back and forth, trying to keep 'em away, but the three of 'em was too many for me. I swung the chain to the right, and the lead dog come in from the left. I didn't even think about it, just whipped the chain as hard as I could at that dog and sent him flying. He didn't get up, and that made give me mixed feelings. I maybe killed a dog, just like Junior done. But it felt good to be safe. That didn't last long, 'cause the next dog come for me. I dashed the chain back the other way and give him such a clip on the shoulder, he slunk off crying into the woods.

The last one wasn't giving up. He started to circle me, but I kept my back to the house and begun sliding toward the way I first come. He'd lunge for me, I'd swing the chain, and he'd jump away. We kept going like that, him lunging and me swinging, 'til I was on the side of the house nearest my truck. But that was all the way across the yard to the road and up the hillside. If I was gonna make it, I had to get that dog, so he wouldn't chase me.

I leaned against the house, swinging the chain back and forth just enough to keep him off. Then I come away from the house and bluffed like I was going to the left. That ol' dog fell for it and come running round to get me. He jumped like he might be going for my throat, and I lashed that chain at his legs. Then I jerked for all I was worth, and he went down. I started to running and never looked back. Maybe I broke his legs, maybe he couldn't free hisself. Didn't know which, but he didn't come after me, and I run up that hillside like I was a track star.

Got in the truck and laid down on the bench seat, knees up and trying to get my breath. Felt like it was burning my lungs, every breath I took, but every breath was also a sign I was still alive. Later on, I felt regret at what I done to them dogs, but not then. I just laid there, my hand on my throat and thanking the Lord it wasn't ripped out.

27

WHEN I GOT HOME, MOM was out with the kids somewhere in our old station wagon. So I put my smelly clothes in the washing machine and hung 'em up over the stove to dry. Told her I slipped and fell in the mud out at Miz Simmons' place and didn't want her to have to clean up after me. She give me a peculiar look, but it was almost supper time, the kids was squawking about being hungry, and she had a lot on her mind. For which I was most thankful.

Hardly slept a wink, my brain was whirling round so much. Thinking how I nearly been shut under that house for the night. Even worse, I mighta been killed by Junior's dogs. Thinking about what I heard while I was under there and if it meant anything. Thinking even more about my Sunday School lesson the next day. Got up at six feeling like I been beat up good but knew I had to pull myself together and do my best with Psalm 121. Repeated it to myself under the shower and while I was getting dressed, so by the time I was driving the family to church, I felt like I was as ready as I'd ever be.

We got outta the car, and I looked for Eden and her momma and baby brother, but they musta already gone in. Mom smiled up at me with her eyes. "You'll do fine," she said and marched the kids off to their own Sunday School classes and herself to adult Bible Study.

I stood in the parking lot a couple minutes after they was gone. The wind'd died down, but it was still cold and gray. Started shivering and didn't know if it was the weather or nerves. Thanked the Lord none of our kids was in junior high yet. No way I coulda taught Sunday School with them in the room.

I found Pastor Bob in the Junior High Class, talking to the regular teacher. "Jimmy Lee," he said and shook my hand, "The Lord and I have faith." Then he was gone, and Miz Christie was introducing me to the class, saying I had the Call and was gonna teach Sunday School that morning.

My mouth was so dry, felt like I couldn't open it. Tried to swallow, but there wasn't nothing there. Looked at Miz Christie, feeling ready to give up. She smiled and nodded her head like she was eager for me to start. So I tried again and managed to say, "Psalm 121. Let's open our Bibles to Psalm 121 and read it out loud together."

That part went pretty good. Everybody seemed all wrapped up in the reading. Then the door opened, somebody motioned to Miz Christie, and she slipped away.

"Anybody here ever feel close to the Lord when you're up in the hills?" I asked, and several of the kids nodded their heads. My heart rose up. This was really going good.

"Who'd like to tell us about that?" My heart sunk. No one volunteered. They all hung back and looked anywhere but at me. "Tell us what makes you feel that way," I said.

A boy at the back put up his hand. He was bigger'n most of the kids and maybe older. He grinned. "Well," he looked round at the other boys in the back, "that kinda depends on what girl I'm with." Them boys all laughed like it was the dirtiest joke they ever heard, nudging each another and winking.

Just then Miz Christie come back, and they all settled down. I wasn't gonna give up on them kids or myself, so I pointed at one of the girls in the front and asked, "You nodded your head about feeling close to the Lord up in the hills. Can you tell us about it?" But the boys at the back started snickering, and she just blushed and hung her head.

I looked at Miz Christie, and she looked at me like it was all up to me to do something. But I couldn't think what to do. I eyed the notes I made on my pad of paper like they was a lifeline. And they was, 'cause I managed to say, "I always think Psalm 121 was written with West Virginia in mind. There's proof of the Lord all round us."

The kids started looking sideways at each other, and a couple of 'em looked out the window. I was starting to feel desperate. "I look at them hills, and I know the Lord is gonna take care of me," I said. "He won't let harm come to me. Not this day, not tomorrow, not ever."

And that's the way it went. Me blabbing on and on, the boys at the back snickering, and the kids at the front looking like they couldn't wait to get outta there.

Finally, Miz Christie stepped in. "I know we all want to thank Jimmy Lee for sharing his faith with us. How about we sing him our favorite hymn?" She smiled at the girl in the front row who'd nodded but didn't talk. "Carrie, you want to lead us?"

Carrie started to sing, and everybody joined in. Except the tall boy in the back. He just smirked at me like he'd won one. And I guess he had. To this day, I have no idea what hymn they sung.

Don't know how I got to the top of the hill behind the Church, but I did. Found myself up there, saying Psalm 121 over and over like it was something magic could make me feel right. Down below, I could hear 'em singing the opening hymn of Sunday Services. But up where I was, up where I was supposed to feel close to the Lord, all I could feel was numb.

I didn't have the Call. Who was I kidding? I couldn't even teach a simple Sunday School lesson. All my work for nothing. Forgot everything I meant to do, all the advice from Pastor Bob and the help from Eden. She'da done a better job than me. She understood what Pastor Bob meant, and she laid it all out for me. But I couldn't do it to save my soul.

What was I gonna tell Mom? What was I gonna say to Pastor Bob? What would Miz Christie tell him? How big a failure I been? Decided I better do that myself and went on down the hill, snuck in church and set in a back pew, not hearing a word 'til the whole Services was over, and we all stood up. Pastor Bob passed me on his way to the door to shake hands. He give me a look and raised his eyebrows, but I held my face still. Eden and her momma walked by, but I held back, and they didn't see me. Mom come near with the kids, looked deep in my eyes and seemed to know now wasn't the time to say or do anything.

Finally, everybody was outta the church, and Pastor Bob walked back in. He come right over to where I was standing, probably looking as hangdog as I felt. "Jimmy Lee? What happened?"

I couldn't speak. Just stood there, head down, wagging it back and forth, trying not to cry.

Pastor Bob drew me down to sit in the last pew. "It didn't go as well as you hoped?"

I shook my head.

"Want to talk about it?"

I nodded, but I couldn't find my voice.

He put a hand on my shoulder. "Tell you what. You take your mother and the kids on home, have your Sunday dinner and come back. We'll talk then. That sound about right?"

I nodded, and he took my hand in both of his. "Whatever happened, it's not the end of the world," he said. "The Lord doesn't give us burdens we can't carry."

Mom had the grace not to say a thing all the way home. She give us a meal of rabbit with boiled potatoes and lima beans. Bread pudding for dessert, cinnamony with raisins. The kids knew something was wrong, but they took their cue from her and kept silent. After lunch, they changed clothes and went out to play. Guess they figured cold and gray outside was better'n me cold and gray inside.

Mom come over and put her arms round me. I stood like that for a while, taking comfort from her silence. She stepped back with her hands holding my arms and looked up into my eyes. "Jimmy Lee, don't ever forget how much the Lord loves you. And your momma too." Then she went to wash up, and I drove back to see Pastor Bob.

No point in going over all the things we said. The bottom line is I was strong about the Lord letting me know I didn't have the Call. And that was the end of it. Pastor Bob followed me out to the truck, laid a hand on the open door after I was inside and said, "The Lord is calling you to do something. We just have to listen better."

All the way home, the tears I been holding back was running down my cheeks.

28

THE ONLY WAY I COULD THINK how to get through the pain was to concentrate on Lazarus and Miz Simmons dying. I been to the Flints' farm and listened to 'em talk about how Junior's boils got cured. That was more grist to the mill, even if I heard it before. But what about Hank Conner and Orrin Dent?

Decided to tackle Orrin first. What he been looking for in them ashes? What he have to hide? And where would he hide it? I had no idea where he lived, but I knew where his pot field was. And no police helicopters ever flew over, so I didn't have to worry about that. Bright and early Monday morning, I got some leftover fence outta the barn and drove out to me and Miz Simmons' place. Parked the truck by the mended fence and went to work to give it a permanent fix.

All the while, I was looking round, trying to see any sign of Orrin being up at his field. The cut fence was across from the old lumber road he used. There wasn't no fresh tire tracks, so he couldn't be up there right then. I finished the fence, drove my truck down, left it inside the gate, put the remote in my pocket and hiked back. Kept to the side of the muddy lumber road, so I wouldn't leave no footprints easy to see.

I never been up there before, but I had a general idea where it was. It took a while and a bunch of breath to get there, but I finally found what I was looking for. Sure enough, Orrin put up one of them greenhouses like I heard he done. Kind that's plastic stretched over bowed rods to hold it up. That plastic wasn't clear, kinda cloudy instead. But I could still see green plants through the milky-looking stuff.

There was pine trees all round, so the whole thing was hid pretty good. A cardinal flew past and took my attention for a second. He landed in one of them trees, bright red against the dark green. I pulled my eyes back to that thin plastic stretched over rods. How was Orrin keeping his plants warm in December? I looked for smoke from a stove, but I didn't see none.

I went round to one end and found a wood door. With a padlock, so no way I was gonna get inside. Unless I slit the plastic. He slit my fence, so was it okay for me to cut open his greenhouse? Lazarus was gone, so cutting open the fence didn't hurt much. Slitting Orrin's greenhouse in winter could cost him his crop. I knew growing pot was wrong, but I didn't wanna mess with a man's livelihood. On the other hand, maybe Orrin fired the cabin, killed Miz Simmons and shot at me. If he did, I didn't owe him any consideration whatsoever.

I got out my penknife, ready to make the smallest slit possible, when I heard a twig crack. Down the trail but way too close for comfort. I didn't even try to peek round the greenhouse and see who was coming. Backed into the pine trees and headed down the ridge as fast as I could with as little noise as possible. Right through the trees, away from the logging track.

Wasn't long before I heard Orrin shout, "Goddam! I know who you are, and I'll make you sorry you ever come up here."

Kept going down the hill, angling toward where my truck was, straining to hear if somebody was running behind me. When I got to the paved road, I stopped to listen, but I didn't hear nobody crashing through the brush behind me. I run as fast as I could to the gate, opened it with the remote, jumped in the truck and hit the highway going full-tilt.

Looked in the rearview mirror, expecting to see Orrin's truck any minute, but all I saw was empty asphalt.

No way I wanted to go back over the ridge to Lewiston and pass the lumber road up to Orrin's field. So I drove the long way home. Almost got there when I spotted a truck slid off the road and into the ditch. Closer I got, I realized it was Mitch's, and he was inside, head slammed against the steering wheel.

Oh Lord, I thought, how bad can it be?

I pulled up in front of his truck, got out and went back to see what I could do. Opened the door and felt my nose wrinkle from the smell of beer so strong it almost made me gag. Blood from Mitch's forehead was running into his eyes, and he was moaning. Knocked out but starting to come to.

"Mitch? Mitch? Wake up now. We gotta get you outta here before the cops come."

I found a near-empty can of beer on the floor and used it to wet my handkerchief and wipe off his face. There was a cut above his eyebrow, where he'd hit the steering wheel, but it didn't look so bad he'd have to go to the hospital. Thank God. They woulda had to tell the cops for sure.

"Come on now, Mitch. Come on. We gotta get you home."

His head lolled round and up at me. "Jimm' Lee. Wha' happened? My head hurts bad."

"You been in a wreck, and we need you to get in my truck, so I can take you home."

He started to get outta his truck, but his legs wouldn't work right, and I caught him just in time. I put his arm over my shoulders and half-drug him to my truck. Got him in the passenger side, found a clean rag and told him to hold that tight against the cut to stop it bleeding.

Then I went back to see if I could get his truck outta the ditch. Things didn't look too bad, so I decided to give it a try. Backed it up a bit to get it straightened out, then put it in first and eased up on the clutch. Truck fishtailed some, but I managed to get it back up on the road. Drove on down aways, so the ruts outta the ditch wasn't near enough for folks to make the connection. That truck didn't look any worse'n a lotta 'em round Lewiston, so I put a sign on the windshield, "Gone for gas," locked it up and headed back to my truck.

Mitch was leaning against the side window, holding the rag against his head and kinda wailing. I couldn't understand a word he said, but I got us outta there and back to his house. I half-drug him inside, cleaned him up with soap and water, closed the cut with adhesive tape and put a bandage over it. Got him in bed and went through that house from front to back, looking in every cupboard and closet. Fridge too. Took every ounce of booze I could find and flushed it down the toilet. Found a baggie of pills in a drawer and flushed that too. I give Mitch three aspirin with a glass of water and told him to stay put 'til I got back, or the cops'd get him for sure.

"Sure thing, Jimm' Lee. You gonna make ev'thing all righ'."

"Not if you don't do your part. Stay in bed and wait for me."

He tried to salute, but he couldn't really pull it off. "Okey dokey. Will do. Ten-four."

I lit outta there and over to PayLo. Borrowed the tow truck without too many questions being asked, and thanked the Lord my old boss trusted me. Left my truck there, towed Mitch's back to his house and returned the tow truck to PayLo. Kinda complicated, but I couldn't work out any other way to get his truck to his house and not leave mine alongside the road.

Then I went on home and got The Big Book from my room. I hadn't had time to read all of it, but I'd read enough. Hurried back to Mitch's house and found him snoring away. I guessed that was the best I could hope for, so I put The Big Book beside him on the bed, open to Bill's story and tiptoed out.

Started to drive away, and it come to me there wasn't nothing to eat or drink in Mitch's fridge. So I went over to Poultry Pantry, got some fried chicken with greens and mashed potatoes. Figured he could eat the first two even if they was cold. Heck, he'd probably eat the mashed potatoes cold too. Bought a bottle of sweet tea and circled back to Mitch's place. He was still snoring, so I put the food and tea on the bedside table, checked that Bill's story was still easy to find and took my leave.

Sure been a bad week, and only two days gone.

29

I LAID IN BED THAT NIGHT and thought about next steps for finding out who killed Miz Simmons. Sure, I heard them Flint brothers talk about how her being burned up cured Junior's boils. But I already knew they thought that. I been silly to think they'd say something to prove they was guilty while I listened in. I needed to goad everybody into action.

Looked like I mighta done that with Orrin. He said he knew who it was and he was gonna make the prowler sorry he was ever up there. If he really knew it was me, he'd be doing something soon enough. Maybe I provoked Junior too. What did he think when he got home and found his dogs busted up, maybe even killed? Would he think it was me? But he was the kinda guy to rush out and do something right then, not wait round all this time. Then I come to Hank Conner. I hadn't done much, if anything, to prod him. So how was I gonna get him to show his hand?

Fell asleep worrying them thoughts back and forth. When I woke up, the Lord give me the answer. I needed to go talk with Mae about Conner. Bethanne'd probably be there too, and she been full of ideas before. Besides, Eden was in her exam week, and there was no way I could ask her advice. She didn't even want a ride back and forth to school. Said she needed to keep her mind on her studies.

Once I made sure Mom didn't need me that morning, I took off for Gifts-n-Such. Sure enough, Mae and Bethanne was there, even though the shop was still closed. I knocked on the door, and Mae come to open it up.

"You're a sight for sore eyes. Come on in. We're gonna have coffee and cake before we start the day." She give me a grin that lit up her whole face. "And we sure need you to help us out."

So we traipsed into the back room where a fresh coffee cake was waiting for us. I swear Mae oughta open a bakery. Nobody makes goodies like her. Not even Miz Stealey. But a while back, Mae told Eden she was through cooking for other folks after the rich lady she worked for was killed. That was part of the mystery that brought Eden and Bethanne and Mae together.

Anyhow, we all set there in the back room of Gifts-n-Such, eating our fill and swapping the news. Bethanne started off, "I don't know if you noticed, but I started recovering on the outside from that attack long before I could recover on the inside. Truth to tell, I'm still not back to being my old self. Maybe I never will."

Once she mentioned it, I realized she been kinda down, and I felt shamed to think I been too focused on myself to pay attention, let alone done anything to help. I tried to say something like that, but she raised her hand to stop me and went on. "I think you know Eden's momma and I got to be friends while Eden and I were solving that mystery." Bethanne rested her cast on the table, and that seemed to ease her some. "Well, Corrine Jones came while I was laid up, and we had a real heart-to-heart. "

I felt kinda flustered and didn't know what to say, so I just nodded my head like I wanted her to go on, which she did. "Corrine invited me to go with her to Pastor Bob's AA Meetings, and they're helping me see I've been causing a lot of my own problems, and booze isn't going to help."

Before I knew it, the dam bust, and I told 'em all about Mitch and how I hoped he'd come to the Meetings too. Bethanne said you gotta get so far down you can't get up without help before you was ready, and I said maybe Mitch's time had come. At least I hoped so.

Bethanne laid her good hand on my arm. "Just remember alcohol's the symptom, not the cause. Your cousin's going to have to find that out like I did."

Mae been watching me the whole time, and she said, "You didn't come just to visit, did you, Jimmy Lee?"

That woman could see through anything, and I told her so. She shook her head, but there was a nice grin on her face. Then I told 'em about how I figured nothing was gonna happen with them suspects unless I made it happen. Told 'em all about being under Junior's house and up at Orrin's greenhouse. But I sure was stumped about how to goad Hank Conner.

They both tried to talk me outta prodding anybody, said it was time to go tell Sheriff Price everything I knew. But I come back with what did I have to tell him? Bethanne reminded me about Miz Simmons' book with the story of what Hank Conner done to her family. Mae looked at Bethanne, shaking her head and frowning, like she was trying to gag her. But it was too late. Bethanne give me an idea, and I couldn't wait to get outta there and put it to work.

Thanked Mae for the cake and Bethanne for her thoughts, said I was going to the library to take out Miz Simmons' book. Left as soon as I could and still be polite. But I wasn't going to no library. Like

I said before, I'm not much of a reader. But I did have me an idea.

I drove out to Gmart and bought a pac of envelopes and some plain white paper. Got a couple copies of the county newspaper and a glue-stick. Already had some old scissors in the truck from Dad always wanting to be ready for anything.

And I was too, ready for anything. Got home and told Mom I had some work to do in the barn. Took all them supplies into Dad's worktbench, cut out words and pasted 'em onto a sheet of white paper. Folded up the paper and put it in an envelope. Addressed it to Hank Conner at the bank. Drove to the post office, got a stamp and dropped the whole thing in Local Mail.

If all went well, he'd get that message the next day. "I know what you done to Mrs. Simmons' family and what you done to her. You can't escape Judgement Day."

That made it lunchtime, so I went over to the Quik Treat. Got me and Mitch burgers and fries and Cokes, then drove to his house. He was still in bed, but it looked like he been up some, 'cause I found a dirty cereal bowl and a coffee cup in the sink. We set in the living room, eating from styrofoam cartons on his banged-up coffee table and drinking Cokes outta plastic bottles.

Mitch almost seemed like his old self. At least he wasn't drunk or on pills. "So what's happening with you and Fireplug?" he asked, and I remembered him warning me about Orrin not wanting to be pushed.

I didn't wanna stir up that hornet's nest, so I said, "Haven't seen him in a while." Took another bite of burger and changed the subject. "How you feeling?"

He just shrugged, and I decided to push my luck a little bit. "You gotta clean up your act, or you're gonna kill yourself." He touched the bandage on his forehead, and I took that as encouragement. "You read Bill's story yet?" I asked.

"Not yet," he said, "I got a headache fit to split me in two."

So I got him three more aspirin and a glass of water. He got 'em down and said, "I need more'n that, J.L. Aspirin ain't gonna cut it."

Thought I was gonna lose it, but I managed to say, "You hear what I been saying? If you don't kill yourself, you might kill somebody else."

He got a little whiny then. "But I'm in pain. Big pain."

"Your head or your back?"

He looked kinda surprised. "My head hurts more'n my back." His grin was kinda lopsided. "Maybe that wreck did something, maybe put my back in line again. Like that chiropractor helped Daddy once. Give his back such a wrench, it never hurt again." He leaned against the couch and crossed his arms. "Goddam! Maybe I discovered something. Your back hurts, get yourself in a car wreck. Fix you right up." And he started cackling like a madman.

I was put off by the swearing and almost as much by the cackling, but I saw my opening and took it. "How about we make a deal? You stay off the pills and booze for another twenty-four hours. Just take aspirin if you need it, and we'll see how things go. In the meantime, I'll lay in enough food to get you through, so you don't need to go out, and you can just concentrate on getting better."

He didn't look very happy, so I said, "Can't hurt, might help."

"Okay, okay," he said, like he was trying to get off the subject.

I tried not to read too much into that, but I did change direction. "You wanna come to Christmas dinner? It's only a week away."

He give me one of his old smiles. "That's kind of you, Jimmy Lee, but I'm expected over to my sister's. Don't wanna disappoint the family."

I could appreciate that, so I took my leave and went off to the Busy Bee. Bought him a TV dinner and a salad. Figured he could have more cereal for breakfast but picked up some orange juice too. When I got back, he was snoring in bed again. But he did have his hand on The Big Book.

30

WEDNESDAY, THE SUN FINALLY come out bright and strong after a week of bad weather. I was antsy with waiting for Orrin or Junior or Conner to do something, but I was waiting for nothing.

Needed to keep busy, and besides, I wanted to know how Mitch was doing, so I drove over to his house. He was setting on his faded green couch with The Big Book, and that give me some hope.

But he dashed that as soon as he opened his mouth. "That book ain't got nothing to do with me. Them stories is all about doctors and lawyers, housewives and students. Ain't none of 'em like me. Everything in such hifalutin writing, I can't hardly read it."

That put me down so low, I didn't know what to say, so I left the book where it was and asked if he needed any more groceries. He give me a list, and I went off to the Busy Bee again. I got everything except the six pack. He was mad about me not bringing that, but I didn't care. I went out to the kitchen to put stuff away and spied his keys on a shelf. I took 'em and put 'em under his momma's old hutch, like they mighta fell outta his pocket. Realized doing that was kinda wrong but kinda right too, 'cause I didn't want him driving out to get that six pack.

Nothing to do but go home and take care of my chores. I tried to keep my mind off everything that was vexing me and kept praying to the Lord, but seemed like He didn't hear me. Maybe 'cause I was being tricky, like hiding Mitch's keys and mailing that threat to Hank Conner. Too late to do anything about that, but I asked the Lord's forgiveness for not being straightforward.

Took a chance and called Eden that night. I was missing her something awful. She was still busy with exams, and we had just a short talk about nothing much. Even so, it cheered me to hear her voice.

Thursday was just about the same on the action front, and I was starting to think I was gonna have to do something else if I was gonna get to the bottom of who killed Miz Simmons.

We was all in bed, way after midnight, when light come on so bright, I thought the sun musta come up, and we was all late to start our day. Then I realized ol' Butch was barking to beat the band. We kept him tied up at night, but he sounded like he was gonna break that chain for sure and go after whatever it was.

Jumped up from bed and looked out the window. Course it wasn't the sun. It was a truck with six strong lights shining on our house. At least I thought it was a truck. Mighta been a SUV. They both look alike from the front when you're half-blinded. And I sure was. That truck, or whatever it was, had on its headlights plus a rack of four lights up on the roof.

But who was it? Coulda been Junior or Conner or Orrin. Whoever it was, I wasn't gonna let 'em get away with it, and I run down the hall to Mom's room for Dad's Winchester. She was way ahead of me, met me at the bedroom door with it loaded and ready for action.

"Jimmy Lee, you get on with it, and I'll get the kids to the back of the house."

I know what you might be thinking, but we neither one of us had any idea to call the cops. We was way out in the country, so it'd take forever for 'em to get there. Besides, folks like us don't call the cops unless there ain't no other choice. This was something we could take care of ourselves, and that's what we was gonna do.

I run down to the back door and outside with the rifle, my heart beating so loud in my ears I couldn't hear a thing. Eased round the house, took aim at one of them lights on top of the truck roof and fired off a round. Musta totally missed, 'cause every light was still shining. Took aim again and missed again. Cursed myself for never being much of a hunter and wished Dad been more of one too. Least I coulda got more practice.

A voice come outta the darkness behind all them lights. All high and squeaky, like a girl's. "You think I can't see you, Jimmy Lee? Peeking round the house, barefoot and in your underwear? Hee hee. You couldn't hit a elephant if it come right up to you, put out his trunk and shook your hand." Then this low, evil laugh went on and on while I just stood there feeling shamed and useless.

The lights went out, but I was still blinded. Couldn't get used to the dark that quick. The truck or SUV or whatever it was backed up, turned round and tore off into the night, leaving me trying to figure out whose voice it been. But for the life of me, I couldn't. That voice mighta been high and squeaky, but it sure was a man talking. If nothing else, that deep laugh said so.

Outta the blue, I realized I was like to froze to death. I was shivering, and I felt kinda sick to my stomach. Knew that was nerves as much as it was the dark winter night, but I didn't want nobody else to know.

Went inside, and Mom come down the stairs with a blanket to wrap round me. "Real proud of you, Jimmy Lee," she said. Up above on the landing, I could see the kids looking all big-eyed and scared, even the oldest. She was holding the baby so tight, he started to bawl.

Mom give me a look I'll never forget, mix of pride and sorrow both. "You're a brave boy, Jimmy Lee. You chased that devil away." She started to turn to go up to the kids, but then she stopped in her tracks. She come back and give me a sad little smile. "Said you was a grown man before. Don't know why I said 'boy' just now. You're a brave man, Jimmy Lee."

Well, that brought tears to both our eyes, but I just give her a hug.

She got all the kids calmed down and back in bed, while I made us some hot tea with honey from our bees. Figured we both could use it. She come back down, and we set together in the kitchen, trying to work out who it was and if they was gonna come back. No answer to either one of them questions, but we was in agreement we sure had a lot to thank the Lord for. We stopped then and there, held hands across the table, and Mom prayed out loud for the both of us.

Finally, we was that worn down we had to get ourselves to bed. But I was so worked up I couldn't go to sleep. Felt like I was losing my mind, with all them things gone wrong. Lost without Dad. No one to turn to for advice like he give me. And I wasn't really a man, even if Mom said so. Only been thinking I was, fooling myself and her too. Feeling Eden pull away from me, our summer love maybe just a dream that couldn't last.

For sure I didn't have the Call. Fooling myself again. Couldn't even help Mitch. No way I was gonna solve the mystery of who burned Miz Simmons to death. I put the whole family in danger and couldn't protect 'em. What was I good for anyway? Nothing.

Nothing that mattered. Just worthless and no-count for anything but farm chores and running errands. And not very good at that, neither.

I tossed and turned, sweating in the sheets, even if I been freezing before. Felt like my chest was gonna bust with the burden of how worthless I was. A fool fooling hisself.

Dawn was starting to show when I got down on my knees beside the bed and confessed to the Lord just how prideful I been and how no-count I was. How I thought I could do everything and couldn't do nothing. How I thought I knew everything and didn't know nothing. How I was one sorry son and brother and friend. And how totally lost I was. Lost in the wilderness and no way out. Just lost.

Mom come for me when I didn't show for breakfast. She found me asleep on the floor, wrapped up in the covers I musta pulled off the bed. She got down beside me and rubbed my shoulder through Grammy's quilt. "Jimmy Lee?" I woke up, embarrassed she found me.

"You all right?" she said.

I threw myself into her arms and started to bawl just like my baby brother the night before. "Oh Mom, I ain't no good for nothing. Everything I try, I fail at."

She started rocking us both to and fro. "Hush, hush. We all feel like that sometimes. We can't see the way forward, 'cause all we can see is the mistakes we made when we look back."

She pushed me off some and looked me in the face. "So you know what the answer is?"

I shook my head.

"Just don't look back." She smiled. "Look at this day. What're we gonna do with this day? Ask the Lord to help you learn from your mistakes and to make this day the best day you can."

31

I HEARD WHAT MOM SAID, but I was so far down in the dumps, I just couldn't do it. Did manage my chores that morning, but I wasn't good for nothing else. Couldn't bear to go see how Mitch was doing. Just another failure there. I was so outta touch with the Lord, He couldn't give me an answer. Thought about talking with Pastor Bob, but I couldn't face him. Didn't want to talk with Eden neither, even if it was Friday, and her exams was over that morning. Seemed like I couldn't bear to do nothing.

No matter how hard I tried, it wasn't much of a day. And for sure not much of a week. The worst day of my life since first Dad and then Miz Simmons died. Felt like I should just die myself and get it over with.

Mom fixed us a nice lunch of my favorite things. Fried chicken with mashed potatoes and gravy and applesauce made with brown sugar and cinnamon just like Grammy used to. Mom never said a word, and I didn't neither. But we both knew what she was doing. She was trying to cheer me up, but even that wonderful meal couldn't do the trick.

She got up to clear the table and stopped behind my chair. Put her arms round me and laid her head on top of my head. Didn't say a word, just stayed like that for a while. Then she went on with her chores, and I went out to the barn to at least try to be useful. Decided to clean up Dad's workbench where I left the stuff for the letter I sent to Hank Conner. I started throwing the mess away and felt like I was throwing myself away. All my work to catch a killer for nothing.

Just give that up, I told myself. And then I realized the Lord was talking to me. How many times and how many people had told me to give up trying to figure out who killed Miz Simmons? Eden and Pastor Bob. Mae and Bethanne. All saying tell Sheriff Price and let him take over. Sheriff saying that almost from the beginning. How stubborn I been to think I could solve the mystery and bring that sucker to justice. Only person I been fooling was myself.

I went back to the house and told Mom what I was gonna do.

She give me this sweet smile. "Always knew you was smart, Jimmy Lee."

I drove into town and up to the Sheriff's office, set on a chair in the waiting room for over an hour without complaining. When I finally got in to see Sheriff Price, he give me a hard look and pointed to one of his old scratched-up chairs.

"You come to confess?"

That made my heart jump a little, but now I felt the Lord with me. "Yes, in a way. I come to tell you all the stuff I been holding back. Hoping what I know will help you solve who killed Miz Simmons."

Sheriff leaned back in his chair and put his hands behind his head. "I'm listening."

His face was so stony, no way I could read him. No idea what he was thinking. So I just plowed ahead.

Started at the beginning and told him everything I knew. Miz Simmons' history with Junior and Orrin and Hank. What I done to goad 'em into action. Them lights shining on our house after midnight and me taking a couple shots with that squeaky voice coming outta the night. What Mitch and Betheanne heard Junior say down to the Roadhouse and I heard repeated when I laid under Junior's house. Left out hurting Junior's dogs, though, didn't wanna talk about that unless I had too. Trespassing on Junior's land was bad enough. I ended up with Floyd talking to Junior about gasoline, over and over again.

Sheriff just set there listening, not taking notes or nothing. No tape recorder neither, just listening.

Lord, I thought, what's he thinking? Does he believe me? Does he think I'm some idiot kid messing up what he been trying to do?

Finally I got to the end of everything I had to say. Sheriff leaned his elbows on the desk and said, "You know what you are, Jimmy Lee? You're a damn fool. Junior was stopped for speeding the night you-all were in danger. Had a rack of lights on top of his truck. But he got off with a warning 'cause we didn't know what you know. You're lucky you're alive, boy. Risked your whole family so you could play detective."

I just set there, hanging my head and knowing the truth of what he said.

"You could be in a while lot of trouble yourself," the Sheriff said, and my heart sunk. "Trespassing on Junior's land, shooting at him when he came to your house at midnight. I got bigger fish to fry, and the county doesn't need to spend time and resources on this penny-ante stuff. Your shooting at that truck with lights was self-defense. If any of this comes up at the trial, just tell the truth and why you done it. That'll be the end of it."

He set back and slapped a hand on his desk top. "Here's what you're gonna do. You're gonna go home and leave everything to me. If you so much as speak two words to anyone about all this, I'm gonna arrest you for obstruction of justice. You understand me?"

I nodded, and he said, "Speak up! I want to hear you say it."

So I said, "Yessir, I understand exactly what you're saying, and I'm gonna do it." Jerry Price didn't know it, but I didn't need him to give me no warning. I already learned my lesson.

He stood up. "Now go on home and keep your mouth shut. Won't be long before I'll be calling you back in as a material witness. In the meantime, go on about your business like you don't know a thing."

I started to get up, and he leaned across the desk and smiled. "Not even to that smart girlfriend of yours. You say nothing to nobody."

I give him another "Yessir" and headed out the door, feeling his eyes bore into my back so hard I had a hot spot between my shoulder blades.

Laying down my burden was such a relief, I knew I had to get to the Church of the Holy Light and thank the Lord. And that's what I done. Got down on my knees and thanked the Lord for not abandoning me, for showing me the way. Then I asked Him to keep on doing that, help me find my way after I been so lost. I didn't know where I was going but I trusted Him to show me the path.

I heard footsteps, and course it was Pastor Bob. Held true to my word and didn't tell him a thing about what I told the Sheriff. But we had us a good talk about the Call, and he helped me realize the Call can mean many things. Not just becoming a preacher if you're not suited to it. And I sure wasn't. But you can be a joyful witness for the Lord in all your life, touching others with how you live. Even with Mitch, even if that took a long time. When I got up to go, Pastor Bob give me a hug and said, "I believe in you."

Felt filled with surprise when I answered back, "I believe in myself."

Got home and found the kids already there with supper about on the table. Leftovers from our wonderful lunch. Mom give me a look with her eyebrows about raised up to her hairline. I just nodded, and she knew what I was saying. Everything's gonna be all right, but I can't talk about it.

Eden didn't call, and I didn't feel the need to call her. Normally, we woulda talked at the end of something like her exam week. But I didn't trust her bright mind not to ferret out what I did that day, so I let it go. Felt an empty place in my heart but knew I had to be strong.

32

You know you can't really keep secrets in a small town. By Monday morning, it was all over Lewiston that Sheriff Price brought Junior in for questioning. One of his deputies had too much to drink with some buddies and told it all. Even acted it out. He got fired too. Made me realize if Jerry Price asks you to do something, you better do it, or face the consequences. Glad I managed to keep my mouth shut.

Took all day Saturday and into the night, but in the end, the Sheriff got what he was after. Deputy said the Sheriff started off by going over everything. I realized some of it was what we both knew and some of it I didn't know. Just showed how I wasn't really cut out to dig up all the facts, no matter what.

Sheriff asked Junior if he tried to kill me out at Miz Simmons' place, and Junior said, "If I been trying to kill him, he'd be dead."

Junior swore that wasn't him shooting at me that day, and his brothers later backed him up. Said they'd all been over to Moorestown looking at some hogs to buy. And they had a bill of sale to prove it. With Junior's name on it.

But Jerry Price wasn't done with asking Junior if he was out to get me. Sheriff asked him if he been to our house at midnight just before the Deputy caught him with a rack of roof lights. Junior muttered one word, "Dogs," and clammed up. Sheriff didn't let up on him, went round and round and back and forth, but Junior kept his mouth shut about what dogs had to do with it.

To this day, I dunno what he mighta said. Did he figure out it was me hurt his dogs? He coulda told the whole thing to Sheriff Price and got me in a lotta trouble. Turns out none of them dogs was killed, but they was hurt pretty bad. The only thing I can work out is that Junior thought he was in deep enough over Miz Simmons' death and didn't wanna risk talking about dogs. He didn't want nobody to see the connection between him torturing and killing Lazarus and burning Miz Simmons alive. Anyway, the Sheriff went on and on about that midnight visit, and Junior finally give some flimsy excuse that nobody in the room believed.

What finally turned the tide with Junior was when Sheriff Price brought up how many people heard Floyd talking to him about gasoline, even singing the word over and over. And what was that gasoline for, if not to burn down Miz Simmons' cabin?

Junior set there a long time, saying nothing. Seemed like he had a lot to think about. Finally, the Deputy said, he owned up like a man. "Okay, I done it," he said, and that was the end of it. Junior was going to jail, just like I knew he would ever since that awful day I called 9-1-1.

Sure felt good to know I been right. But I had to chastise myself too. I been thinking Sheriff Price would never do a thing about Junior 'cause they was kin. Maybe he'd look the other way about some things, but not about murder. Had to give him credit for that. When it got serious, Jerry Price done his duty.

Course Junior got a lawyer, one of them volunteers, so he didn't have to pay. But we all figured you get what you pay for, and Junior was going to prison for the rest of his life. He couldn't even afford bail, so he spent Christmas in the regional jail, while his brothers ate turkey and all the trimmings at the Corner Cafe. Then they went to visit Junior. The brothers later told anybody who'd listen what happened, so we all heard the details at least second-hand. They was allowed to sit one at a time in a little booth with glass so they couldn't touch him, just talk through this screened opening.

They took turns going in, the two brothers who worked during the week over on the Ohio River. They talked with Junior about how they was gonna get him off, but he told his brothers to shut up. Said he'd fessed up, and that was that. Floyd couldn't be trusted to go in by hisself, so he set with whichever brother was in the waiting room, singing "Jingle Bells" over and over 'til the brothers couldn't take it no more.

We had us a fine Christmas. Our first without Dad, but me and Mom, we was determined to make it as happy as we could. The whole family went out the week before and found the best tree we could on our land. Cut it down and decorated it with ornaments been in our family for generations. Kids made chains with the white paper I had left over from sending the letter to Hank Conner, and that was a better use of the paper than what I done.

Me and Mom wrapped all the kids' presents we got at Gmart, and you never saw such joy as my brothers and sisters had that day. I even managed to sneak Mom's comforter under the tree without her seeing. I was scared she'd be mad that I went ahead and did what she told me not to, so I said, "You can keep Dad's blanket next to you with this on top."

She been holding her head down, and she looked up and said, "Your Dad be so proud of the man you turned out to be." We both got kinda red in the face from holding back our feelings, but that was okay.

Mom had something for me too. She been knitting me a sweater for weeks without my knowing. All that handwork she done in the evenings was so she could knit when I wasn't to home during the day. Every time I went out, she worked on it some 'til it was done and so fine I knew it'd be just for church.

Course we all went to church on Christmas. Bethanne and Miz Jones come in together, and I saw a peace on Bethanne's face that hadn't been there since the night she been beat up. That give me a feeling of warmth for her, and how brave she was to keep going, no matter what. Then I saw Eden and felt my heart jump. I tried to keep cool, 'cause I wasn't sure what was gonna happen. She come up to me and give me a big hug. "Merry Christmas, Jimmy Lee. You sure have a lot to be thankful for this day."

Pastor Bob preached a fine sermon about the promise God made to his children on Christmas Day, but I couldn't help but keep looking over at Eden. She musta had on what she got for Christmas too. A red sweater that made her face glow and a red headband holding back her beautiful long hair. I set there looking at her, wondering what her hug and words meant. Maybe I been getting upset over nothing.

I been thinking she was drawing away. But maybe she just had a lot on her plate and needed to take care of it. She wanted to go to college, and she had to study hard. We wasn't together as much as we used to be, and I missed that something fierce. But maybe I got that all wrong. Now her studying was over for the holidays, maybe we could spend time together. Sure made me happy to think that. And happy to realize that red neck scarf I brought along was gonna be the right thing after all.

Finally I got my mind back to Pastor Bob's sermon just as he was saying, "For God loved the world so much that he gave his only Son, so that everyone who believes in him may not die but have eternal life." Pastor Bob stretched his arms wide, embracing all the congregation and smiled. "My friends, that's the Good News of Christmas."

Afterwards, me and Mom and the kids went up to Mitch and his sister and all her family and give 'em big hugs. Except for Mitch. He got gentle hugs 'cause of his back. Mom thanked 'em for the deer meat and said it was gonna get us through the winter. Then we all went into the Social. So many folks was swapping presents there, no one seemed to notice when I give mine to Eden. Had it all wrapped up too. Used some of the paper and ribbon leftover from the kids' gifts. She give me a hug and a kiss on the cheek, but she didn't have no present for me. Said she didn't have time to do no Christmas-shopping, but I noticed Miz Jones was wearing a nice new blouse, and I couldn't help wondering. Then I told myself the point of Christmas is to give gifts the way the Wise Men give gifts to the Christ Child. And I was shamed to think I been looking to get one.

The next day, I dropped by to see Mitch and found him setting on the couch, watching the TV. He was mostly healed up from the wreck. His back wasn't hurting too bad, so he was off the pills. But still on the booze. Well, beer really. I figured it wouldn't do no good to talk about six packs, so I set a spell and gossiped.

He already heard about Junior and said, "Couldn't happen to a nicer guy," meaning getting locked up at Christmas time. Not a very Christian thing to say, but I could see where he was coming from.

We set there awhile, watching "Challenge." These guys was trying to win this weird game with tilting platforms and slick climbing poles. They kept falling off into muddy water, even though it seemed like they was real fit. Felt like old times, watching the TV with Mitch, before all our misery come upon us. That was a pretty good visit, all in all, and it give me hope maybe Mitch was gonna turn the corner.

33

SPRING COME EARLY THAT YEAR, daffodils peeking through patchy snow, pears in bloom, creeks running high and fast. Wasn't long before Junior's trial date come up. Despite him telling the Sheriff he done it, his lawyer was having him plead Not Guilty. Maybe Junior thought there'd still be a way out. Anyway, his lawyer said Junior been hassled for fifteen hours without having no lawyer there, so when he confessed, it wasn't fair or right. The judge ruled Junior's confession could be admitted as evidence, but it was up to the jury whether to believe it or not. He said they should pay close attention to the rest of the evidence and the arguments from the County Prosecutor and Junior's lawyer. The judge was real careful about how the lawyers picked folks to be on the jury. He didn't want nobody who could be influenced by connections to Junior or his kin.

I was summoned to be a witness for the county, so I wasn't allowed to watch the trial. But just about everybody I knew went as much as they could. Mitch took off from work to be there everyday. Made me feel bad, him missing work when construction jobs had started again, but he said he had some cash saved up, and he wanted to see the whole thing. Mr. Farnsworth come to watch when he could. Bethanne and Mae took turns, so there was always somebody minding the store. None of 'em was allowed to tell me what happened during the trial, and we all did our best to abide by that. But after the trial was over, they give me all the details they could.

Course Eden was in school, so she didn't go to the courthouse. Sometimes we'd meet for a Coke in the late afternoon, not to talk about the trial, but just to have us a visit. I could tell she knew what was going on at the courthouse, but it felt like she wasn't real interested. Seemed like most of her mind was elsewhere, but she didn't say what. So we'd sit and drink our Cokes and talk about stuff that didn't matter much to either one of us. Who was dating who, how the kids didn't respect some teacher, things like that.

At the courthouse, Mitch always set in the narrow balcony above the main floor, so he could see everything. Just a couple rows and folding wood chairs like to cripple your rear end, he said, but it had the best view. Hot up there, all the heat from the radiators getting trapped, but he was determined to stick it out. He saw Hank Conner and Orrin Hatch setting in the ground floor seats most days, so they clearly wasn't involved in the trial no matter what they done.

Junior set down below at the defense table, lounging back in his chair like he didn't have nothing to worry about. Or that's what he wanted everybody to think, how cool he was about the whole thing. Becky Phillips come everyday to set in the gallery with their baby, but Mitch said Junior never turned even once to give her a glance. She looked like Death already come near, he said, that pretty girl become middle-aged overnight.

All Junior's brothers set in the spectator chairs on the other side of the rail behind him. Guess they took off work to lend him their support. They brought Floyd too, probably couldn't leave him home with nobody to watch over him. He got excited now and then and tried to talk, but they shushed him, and he minded pretty good. Bet they give him a talking-to at home to help him understand how he had to behave.

Mitch said the Prosecutor sure had his act together. Took the jury through all the evidence from start to finish. When my turn come, I think I done okay. Took all morning, starting way back with how Miz Simmons come to save Lazarus and Junior killing that wonderful dog and her cursing Junior right then and there. The hard part was telling about her being burned to death, and I almost choked to get the words out. But the Prosecutor took his time and was gentle with me. Which is more'n I can say for Junior's lawyer. He did his best to twist me up every which way, but I asked the Lord to keep me calm, and it was like He sent an angel to stand beside me. That lawyer couldn't get me rattled no matter how hard he tried.

I wasn't allowed to tell what folks heard Junior saying down to the Roadhouse about Miz Simmons, but the Prosecutor had witnesses for that. I did get to tell about Floyd going on and on about gasoline, and there was other witnesses to that too. Finally, the Prosecutor asked me to tell about laying under Junior's house and hearing him say, "That witch burning up is what cured my boils."

Course the defense lawyer had a field day with me trespassing, but I told it honest. Said "Yessir, I know I done wrong to do that, but I wasn't thinking about it at the time. Only thing on my mind was trying to find out who killed the woman who treated me like family." I looked over at the jury, and a couple of 'em nodded their heads like it made sense to 'em. Thank the Lord Junior didn't bring up nothing about his dogs, so his lawyer couldn't question me about that.

Later on, I was called back to tell about somebody coming out to our house in the dead of night, and a deputy testified that they stopped Junior for speeding nearby in a truck with a rack of lights. Turned out there was more about all that in Junior's confession. He wrote he was just sick of me following him round and asking questions about him, so he wanted to teach me a lesson. Anyway, it was going to be up to the jury to believe his confession or not.

Course the Prosecutor didn't bring up me getting shot at, 'cause Junior had proof he was in Morristown with his brothers that day. Problem was him and the Sheriff didn't really have strong proof of anything, just "circumstantial evidence," which is what Junior's lawyer called it. He made a real good case for the jury ignoring "all those little stories." But it felt to Mitch and all my friends like the Prosecutor done an even better job of pulling all them details together.

Most amazing thing was Junior's lawyer didn't call on him to testify. Just made his case and kept Junior out of it. I guess that could cut two ways. Either Junior's lawyer thought so much of hisself that he'd make it obvious Junior was innocent. Or the lawyer didn't trust Junior to testify and answer the Prosecutor's questions without proving hisself guilty. Anyway, Junior didn't say a word at his own trial.

The jury was out three long days. Didn't know what to do with myself, so I ended up setting in the Corner Cafe most of the time. Everybody there was talking about the trial, but I just kept mum. Didn't wanna risk saying something that might get me in trouble with the court. I was going to be allowed back in to hear the verdict, and that meant the world to me.

Mr. Farnsworth come in for a cup of coffee, and I did ask him about physical proof and what they called "circumstantial evidence." I was worried about 'em not finding no fingerprints or gas cans or anything like that.

"Jimmy Lee," he said, "you know I can't talk to you about the actual trial." I nodded, and he went on, "But I can talk about these things in general. Very often, if there's enough of it and it holds together, circumstantial evidence can be more damning than physical evidence. It's like pieces of a puzzle. You get enough of them, you can figure out the rest." He stood up and patted my shoulder. "Try not to worry," he said and walked away.

Finally, somebody come running from the courthouse to the Corner Cafe to shout that the jury brought in a verdict. Just about everybody got up and started running back. Panting and elbowing some, if truth be told. Seemed like the whole town wanted to be there. I rushed up to the balcony. Mitch was saving me a seat right by the rail, so I could see everything down below.

Junior set lounging on his backbone with one elbow over the back of the chair. His brothers was close behind, leaning forward like they wanted to touch him if they could. Course Junior had to stand when the foreman give his verdict. And when the word come down, he didn't move a muscle, just took it like a man. "Guilty."

Floyd jumped over the railing and into Junior's arms, his voice like a banshee shriek. "No, no, no, no, no. I done it." He was holding onto his brother and begging. "You know I done it. I told you right after. That old witch put a hant on you, and I took it off. Gasoline! Gasoline!"

You never saw such a hullabaloo. Everybody talking at once. Judge banging his gavel for order. Junior's lawyer asking the verdict be set aside. Jurors looking like they just passed through the gates of hell.

Junior stood there, his arms tight round Floyd, stroking his hair, whispering, trying to get him to hush up.

I set in my chair, looking down on that scene, and I realized Junior's face was wet with tears. That's when it come to me I been wrong all along. Floyd done it, and Junior been protecting him. Just like he done all Floyd's life.

34

Took months, but everything got sorted out. The judge set aside the verdict and directed the Prosecutor to look into Floyd's confession and report back. More they got into it, the more they realized Floyd wasn't trying to save Junior, he really done it. Floyd give a lotta facts, real proud of hisself about how he carried the gas cans one by one down near to Miz Simmons' and hid 'em under some logs 'til he had enough to do what he wanted. Then he strung a rope through the empty cans and hauled 'em back up the ridge and home before I came. He didn't know if she was in the cabin, but he knew he taught her a lesson she wouldn't forget.

In the end, poor ol' Floyd didn't have the wits to work with no lawyer. County had a shrink check him out, and Floyd didn't really understand Miz Simmons was dead. Thought you burned witches, taught 'em a lesson, and they just up and disappeared. Long story short, Floyd ended up in the State Mental Hospital, so he couldn't be a danger to hisself or to others.

Course Floyd's brothers, and especially Junior, tried to do everything they could to help him, but all the facts kicked into place for the Prosecutor and the Judge. Wasn't nothing Floyd's brothers could do. And maybe once they thought about it, him being in the State Hospital probably was best for all.

Mr. Farnsworth said Junior coulda been charged with being "an accessory after the fact," taking blame and shielding Floyd from the law. But the County Prosecutor decided what was the point in taking him to trial. Besides, Junior been held in jail so long, he already suffered for his sins. We all thought the Prosecutor done the right thing. What good was it gonna do to put Junior in jail for what any of us mighta done? Family is family.

Junior was never the same. The vicious streak that been such a part of his makeup disappeared. Seemed like he didn't have the energy to hurt nobody no more, human or animal either one. Oh, he didn't find Jesus. Didn't come to church on Sunday. He just lost all will to fight. And to be mean to anybody who wasn't family.

I come to see Junior wasn't so no-count after all. Did his best to save Floyd when his brother's weak wits steered him wrong. Tried to take the blame when it seemed like the Sheriff was gonna follow Floyd's "gasoline, gasoline" talk. I had to admit Junior had some virtue after all, deep down where it didn't show 'til he had to call on it. You got to admire that, even if he was wrong. So finally I was able to hate the sin and love the sinner, just like Pastor Bob preaches.

Neither me or Sheriff Price could ever prove who shot at me when I was trying to find clues out where the cabin burned. I'll always think it was Hank Conner. He was sure there, tried to run me off the road when he saw me. That didn't work, so he turned round and got his rifle. Come home with a muddy knee from kneeling down to steady it. Turns out he been a Vietnam Vet, a sniper, so he didn't have no qualms about shooting a man to death. I figure somehow what I done got to him, and he was gonna shut me up. Not the letter I sent him, that was later. But I was following him round and asking questions. I was a friend to Miz Simmons. Doesn't seem like much to you and me, but maybe that was enough for a man so vain he couldn't bear for folks to think less of him than he thought of hisself. Whatever it was, the Lord reached down to keep me safe. Have to think God already had in mind what He wanted me to do, but I was too busy following my own selfish plan to pay attention.

No idea, either, why Orrin and maybe somebody else was sifting through the ashes after Miz Simmons cabin burned. Did they think "that ol' widder woman" had diamonds that survived the fire? If they did, they sure got fooled. Never saw Miz Simmons wear anything but her gold wedding band and the watch her dad give her when she graduated from college.

Once all the hoo-ha was over, the town settled down to normal life again. And I did too. Taking care of chores, helping Mom raise the kids, getting our farm in order, trying to be patient for the will to get probated.

I didn't take Eden to school every morning and pick her up every afternoon. We was past that, each of us with things to do. But we got together now and then, had us a Coke and a talk, catching up on each other's news. I'd run my plans by her, and she always had good suggestions for how to make things better. Round about September, it finally come to me we was just good friends, not boyfriend and girlfriend no more. Been a long time since we kissed, but we hugged a lot, and I always felt her on my side, ready to buck me up if I needed it.

When I finally realized our sweet first love was over, I was laying in bed with the moonlight streaming through the window onto

Grammy's old quilt. I raised up my head and looked at all them patterns she cut and sewed and all the love went from her hands into that quilt. I realized then that Eden was never gonna do that for our own family, and peace come down to soothe me. It was okay, 'cause we would always love each other. Just not the way we did, and not the way I thought we would.

More'n a year went by after Miz Simmons died before her will was probated. I was just barely eighteen, but that was enough for me to be an adult. Mr. Farnsworth done all he could to move the whole thing along, and the Lord rewarded him for his hard work. He called and asked me to come into his office for the paperwork. I let out a holler when I got off the phone and run to give Mom a big hug. All our money worries was over for good. There was Miz Simmons' cash in the bank and royalties coming from the books plus the land out where the cabin used to be. Mr. Farnsworth had paid the property taxes for a year, so I didn't even have to do that.

"All you have to do," he said, "is be a good steward of all she left."

And be thankful, I thought. Soon as I left his office, I knew what I had to do. Drove out to me and Miz Simmons' place—still didn't feel like mine yet. Maybe it never would. Maybe it would always be our place. Anyway, drove out there and got down on my knees back where her and Lazarus's ashes was. Ground was wet and seeping through my jeans, but I didn't even feel that 'til I got back in the truck.

Knelt down there and told 'em my deepest feelings, feelings I hadn't even been able to admit to myself. "I know I let you down, trying to bring your killer to justice. Bounced all over the place with nothing to show for it. But I done my best, and maybe that's all a body can do. Maybe I can learn to forgive myself and move on." I put my hand on the ground where Miz Simmons' ashes was. "Don't know what to do with all you give me, but the Lord will provide the answer, and when He does, it'll be all for you." I put my other hand down. "And Lazarus."

One of the first things I done to be a good steward was go over to Moorestown Livestock and get us a cow and calf. In place of the ones we had to sell to make ends meet when Dad died. Roans, that pretty rust color with white. Made me feel good to go down to the barn and let 'em out to eat the sweet new grass when spring come. Talked with Mr. Farnsworth about raising up that calf so we could sell her and maybe buy more, maybe set up a real cow-and-calf operation one day. He said he thought it was a good idea, and he'd help me with any paperwork I needed.

And that's what I done, worked with Mr. Farnsworth to grow the money Miz Simmons give me. Set up that business at home, so Mom and the kids would have something to depend on. We all of us worked like demons, and first we had beef to trade and then animals and meat to sell. We ain't rich, but we sure don't worry like we used to.

My brothers and sisters never let me and Mom down. Course we did our best to raise them kids right, and it was like Dad was looking down and helping too. Every one of 'em studied hard in school and made good grades. Well, not like Eden, but Bs at least. More'n I can say for myself. My next youngest brother got a 4-H scholarship to the University Ag School and went on to be a county agent. My oldest sister become a nursing assistant, and all of 'em stayed off drugs and booze. Didn't even smoke. Not that I know of, anyway. I'm real proud of how they turned out. Like to think I had a hand in it, and that Dad's up there somewhere, proud of me for how I tried to be the man of the family.

Me and Eden is still friends. Even now, long after them terrible months passed, Eden wears that little heart bracelet I give her. A lotta the silver's wore off, and some kinda cheap metal shows through, but it's still on her wrist. Seems like we're gonna be friends for life, the kind that never, ever lets you down.

Once we got our cattle business going good enough, I started thinking about what I was gonna do with the land Miz Simmons left me. Summer come, insects flying everywhere, heat and humidity like to melt the asphalt. The oldest kids was big enough to take my place at home, at least for the summer, and we could even hire some help when we needed it. So I was freed up to follow what I knew the Lord wanted me to do. Talked it over with Eden, and the first thing she done was reach across the table out at the Quik Treet, put a hand on my arm and say, "That's just so perfect, Jimmy Lee. Go for it."

And I done it. Mr. Farnsworth helped with all the legal and financial stuff, but I done all the rest. Took a while, 'cause I still had things to do at home, but every chance I got, I went out to the land Miz Simmons left me. Cleaned up where the cabin used to be and built me a new one, Mitch helping now and then, just like before. Put up a shelf inside with Miz Simmons' books, but they didn't teach me more about her. They just bring her back close to me when I pick one up. It's like she's telling me stories again, just like she used to.

Outside, I raised up a little white fence round where Miz Simmons' and Lazarus's ashes was. Planted some of her bulbs there too, so she'd have flowers over her grave when spring come. Then I built some pens and shelters and started raising dogs. Out where I found them old bones the first day I ever come to Miz Simmons' place. Just seemed right to put the kennel there. Hired Mitch to help out. He still drinks, but he's coming to church, and I ain't gonna give up on him.

Folks come from miles round to buy my Shepherds. Kept Miz Simmons' Chevy Suburban and put my kennel signs on the side. That makes for good publicity when I drive round, and I can carry my dogs in the back, safe with a grill so they can't jump into the front. Mom says I should name my place "Lazarus." But I feel like I don't need his name on a sign for me to remember him.

Sometimes, at the end of the day, I go set under our sycamore tree on them same old overturned logs we always used. I look up at the hills, and I know I'm where the Lord wants me to be. It's like I can feel Miz Simmons and Lazarus there too. The sun turns the creek into a gold ribbon, and the swallows flash by in one last swoop before they head for their nests. It's so beautiful. And lonesome.

Enough to make a grown man cry.

Questions for Discussion

1. What name do you think Jimmy Lee gave his kennel?

2. Should Junior have gone to jail for trying to protect Floyd?

3. Are you persuaded that Hank Conner shot at Jimmy Lee?

4. What about why Orrin was sifting through the ashes—do you agree with Jimmy Lee's searching-for-diamonds hypothesis?

5. Were you convinced by the reasons given for not calling the cops when crimes were committed? Would you have called them under the circumstances? Why or why not?

6. Most men and boys in West Virginia are hunters. Jimmy Lee isn't much of a shot. How did you feel about that? Was it realistic? Why or why not?

7. Do you think Jimmy Lee didn't really have the Call to work in the church? Did Pastor Bob set him up to fail or did he suggest the Sunday School lesson as an opportunity for Jimmy Lee's self-discovery?

8. If you're male, can you recall any emotions similar to Jimmy Lee's that you experienced in your teens? Which ones? What three adjectives would you use to describe him?

9. Is Jimmy Lee too weepy for a sixteen year-old guy? Why or why not?

10. How did you feel about Eden in the second book of the trilogy? How has she changed? What three adjectives would you use to describe her?

11. Do you think Jimmy Lee and Eden were right to end their romantic relationship without discussing it? And yet they remained supportive friends; how do you feel about that?

12. How did you feel about Bethanne in the second book of the trilogy? How has she changed?

13. What do you think will happen to Jimmy Lee, Eden and Bethanne in the final book of the trilogy?

14. Do you think the characters are stereotypes? Why or why not?

15. Which characters did you most identify or empathize with? Why?

16. Which characters did you have the most trouble understanding? Why might that be?

17. Were you offended by words like "half-wit" and "white trash," or did you see them as words that the character might use?

18. Some readers have said there's too much religion in this book. How do you feel about that?

19. If a scenic but rural and isolated property like Mrs. Simmons' became a possibility for you, would you leap at it or shy away? Why?

20. Have you ever felt powerless in a community or organization where informal relationships among higher-ups were more important than official rules? What happened? Were you able to get around that?

1

"FUCKER'S LYING."

Throughout the blond oak pews, faces turned and glowered. Lips pursed and hissed, "Shhhhhhhh."

Alice Dundee ignored the twinges of arthritis in her hips and swiveled to her left, ready to reprimand the offender.

But Tilda, on his other side, was faster. Alice's friend reached out a wrinkled hand to touch his wrist. "Language, Fred."

"Well, I don't give a good goddam. He's a fucking liar."

Alice inclined her shaggy gray head until her lips were an inch from Fred's hearing aid. "Perhaps he is, but this is not the time. We're here for Lucy."

Out of the corner of her eye, Alice glimpsed Charlie Coleman, another of Lucy's friends from the Evergreen Retirement Community, leaning forward. He set his mouth in a straight line and nodded his head in emphatic agreement.

Alice sat back, smoothed her navy sweater-coat down her lap and focused on Rodney Cunningham. Lewiston's premier property developer was winding up his eulogy in the pulpit of the Southern Baptist Church. He was certainly dressed for the part, she reflected, white shirt gleaming against black suit and tie.

Rodney's fervor filled the air. "I always prayed Lucy and I would be reconciled, and Jesus answered my prayers." He paused to run a hand down the silver of his carefully groomed Van Dyke, as if he might be holding back strong emotions.

"Praise the Lord," said the lady just in front of Fred.

"Hallelujah," said the one behind.

Fred opened his mouth to speak, but Alice put an admonishing finger on her lips. The cloying smell of flowers banked six feet high threatened to turn her stomach, so she forced her attention back to Rodney's oration.

"I knew the Lord was with me when I went into that hospital room. And sure enough, Lucy asked me to get down on my knees."

Fred snorted, and Alice squeezed his fingers so hard he winced.

West Virginia's pale winter sun slanted through a stained glass window and bounced off the bald top of Rodney's head like a halo. "We held hands, and we prayed together." Rodney raised his arms toward the light. "Friends, I felt God take her. He released Lucy from her suffering."

"Thank you, Lord, thank you," said a man across the aisle.

Rodney clasped both hands in front of his chest and bowed his head. "My beloved wife died in the arms of Jesus."

Alice lifted her chin and looked at him through slitted eyes. The perfect picture of a man unable to go on. Probably just the effect he wanted.

Later in the church hall, Alice led Lucy's friends from the refreshment table to some chairs in the corner. "Lucy wasn't religious," Alice said. "She thought religion was a crutch for the weak."

Tilda stopped nibbling at the catered tea sandwich. "Well yes, she did say that, but maybe she didn't really believe it, especially with death near. Could Rodney be right?"

Fred banged his fist down on his wrinkled trousers. "Goddam liar." The retired dentist looked ready to pull every tooth in Rodney's head.

"Lucy was fine when I saw her that morning," Alice said. "Talked about coming home and playing bridge again." She looked around the wainscoted hall, making sure no one was near enough to hear the friends' comments.

Charlie tugged at his collar and tie, clearly uncomfortable out of his usual tracksuit and tennis shoes. "That divorce was final ten years ago, but Rodney wouldn't let go. Wanted his little chippies on the side and Lucy too."

"Kept coming over," Alice said, "getting her so upset, she'd have to take one of her pills." The former math teach looked at each face. The friends seemed to be contemplating just where her words might lead.

Tilda voiced what their faces revealed. "Nearly worried Lucy to death." She adjusted her wire-rimmed spectacles. "Maybe that's what really happened."

"Fucker's lying," Fred repeated. The friends all looked at him, and Alice wondered if his Alzheimers was getting so bad that it wouldn't be long before he couldn't come out in public.

Charlie seemed to have lost patience. "Stop sounding like a broken record." He pointed at Rodney, standing across the room in the midst of a gaggle of admiring women. "Of course he's a liar. We all know that. Question is, what're we going to do about it?"

"Prove it," said Alice.

Made in the USA
San Bernardino, CA
30 March 2019